Turnabout is Foul Play

Clint jumped forward and drove the barrel of his six-gun into Mitch's throat. He cocked back the hammer of his gun. "Now call your overgrown brother and tell him you just found that little girl."

When Mitch hesitated, Clint jammed the barrel of his gun into his throat again, and this time Mitch was a believer. "Hank!" he shouted. "Hank, I found Annie! Come on over here."

They both heard the giant come running. "One word of warning and you're both dead men. Understood?"

Mitch nodded.

The running footsteps slowed to a walk and then stopped altogether. "Mitch, where are you?"

"I'm over here!"

"You got the girl?"

"Yeah," Mitch croaked. "I got her!"

Clint turned around and waited for Hank to appear, but when he did, the Gunsmith had the worst surprise of his life. The muzzle of Hank's Colt was pressed up against Annie's head.

Hank held the wriggling girl against his chest with one massive forearm. "*I* got her, not you. So drop your gun or I'll blow her brains all over these rocks."

Also in THE GUNSMITH series

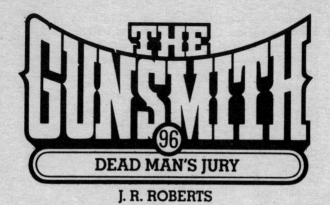

THE GUNSMITH 96

DEAD MAN'S JURY

J. R. ROBERTS

JOVE BOOKS, NEW YORK

DEAD MAN'S JURY

A Jove Book/published by arrangement with
the author

PRINTING HISTORY
Jove edition/December 1989

ISBN: 0-515-10195-8

Jove Books are published by The Berkley Publishing Group,
200 Madison Avenue, New York, New York 10016
The name "JOVE" and the "J" logo
are trademarks belonging to Jove Publications, Inc.

PRINTED IN THE UNITED STATES OF AMERICA

10 9 8 7 6 5 4 3 2 1

ONE

Clint Adams rode slowly up the hot, dusty road as he approached the booming mining town of Candelaria, Nevada. This was hard, dry country, and the Gunsmith could see the outline of Candelaria, which rested in a broad, treeless valley choked with sage and ringed by black lava mountains. Just ahead of him, a desert tortoise struggled slowly across the stage road, grimly determined to vanish into the heavy sagebrush. Other than the turtle, not a damn thing was moving, not even a dust devil.

The Gunsmith had ridden over from Phoenix, and right now he was cussing himself for waiting until late June to cross this hot, sun-blasted desert. His black gelding, Duke, was sweating freely despite the fact that the Gunsmith had let the animal set its own easy pace.

Clint glanced up at the sun. It was still climbing. Candelaria was only a few miles ahead, and it looked to be pretty good sized, so he had few doubts that he could find a barn and water for Duke, and a saloon with a cool beer for himself.

Clint reached into his pocket and pulled out a roll of bills. He counted his money and took some comfort in the fact that he had almost three hundred dollars. He'd probably add to that amount when he gambled in town, but he damn sure would not allow himself to lose, because the money was going to have to carry him all summer while he relaxed and enjoyed himself in the cool Sierra Nevadas.

He was just shoving his money into his pockets when damned if he didn't hear the drumming of hoofbeats coming up fast behind him. The Gunsmith twisted around in his saddle to see four riders galloping up the road, obviously in a hurry to reach Candelaria.

The men were all big and their horses matched their size, but the animals were heavily lathered, and Clint thought the men fools for pushing such fine horses in this heat. The Gunsmith reined Duke over to the side of the road, and the four riders stared at him hard but did not say so much as "go to hell" or "good-bye." The riders didn't even slow down.

They galloped right over the top of the poor tortoise, and that made Clint mad. He trotted up to the creature, which had been knoced over onto its back and was now waving its legs at the hot sun. A tortoise would die within an hour upside down like this in the heat, so Clint dismounted and turned it over. The grateful tortoise ducked its bullet-shaped head inside its shell, and Clint carried it over to the sage and set it free. He watched for a full minute before the tortoise jammed its head out of its shell and then lurched into the brush to disappear.

Clint remounted his horse, pulled up his neckerchief because of the cloud of dust left by the four riders, and continued toward Candelaria.

"Damn fools," Clint muttered. "What the hell is the big hurry on a day like this?"

Unbeknownst to the Gunsmith, the leader of the four riders had almost pulled his gun, but at the last moment had decided that they were too close to Candelaria, and that the gunshot might be heard and alert the town to trouble.

"He'll remember us, Mitch! He saw our faces."

"It don't matter," Mitch hollered, loud enough for all three of his brothers to hear over the drumming hoofbeats of their horses. "Somebody in town is going to recognize us anyway. Ain't no hiding the fact that the Pike brothers have taken the outlaw trail. You want to wear a hood in this heat, go right ahead. I say the hell with it."

"I want the young women to see my pretty face!" Jud Pike hooted. "I want to be more famous than Billy the Kid."

Jud was the youngest. He was proud, lean, and hotheaded. Like his three brothers, he was over six feet tall, broad-shouldered, and handsome, with sharp features, oil-black hair, and prominent cheekbones.

Hank Pike was the giant of the family, but he was dimwitted and mean, while Ulysses was the most deadly, a man so uncommonly fast with a gun or knife that he made even his own brothers nervous when he was on the prod.

The four brothers were in a big hurry. At ten o'clock, the Bank of Candelaria had opened for business, and it was now nearing eleven o'clock, the hour when Candelaria's bank manager always opened his vault. And down at the Wells Fargo stage building, the mine payroll would be ready for shipment.

Hell, Mitch Pike thought with a confident grin, the only unknown about what they were about to do in Candelaria was which one of the two establishments would be forced to hand over the most money.

When they reached the outskirts of town, Mitch pulled his horse to a walk, and his brothers closed in beside him. Mitch wasn't the biggest of the Pike brothers, or the strongest, or even the fastest with a gun but he was recognized as the smartest and the most level-headed. Those attributes, coupled with the fact that he was in his early thirties while his brothers were all in their twenties, had earned Mitch the right to be leader.

"All right," he said. "We've gone over the plan enough times that there should be no questions. Hank and I will take the bank; Ulysses and Jud will hit the Wells Fargo office. We stay inside both buildings until we're all finished, then we come out at the same time, and there had better not be anyone coming out after us. Make sure everyone is bound and gagged so we've got time to get a five- or ten-minute head start before the town even realizes it's been robbed. Any questions?"

"What if we have to shoot to kill?" Jud said, sleeving the sweat from his face. "If a man pulls a gun on me, I'm sure as hell not going to stand and smile at him."

Mitch stared hard at his youngest brother. "If you have to kill a man, do it with your knife. One shot will alert the whole town."

"Who cares?" Ulysses, the deadliest of them, asked. "The townspeople are nothing but a bunch of miners and storekeepers. We've been here often enough to know that there ain't even a sheriff anymore, since I shot the last one."

"No gun play!" Mitch repeated sharply. "I'm telling you, this might not be as easy as we expect. Sometimes people will surprise you. Any sonofabitchin' storekeeper can stick his shotgun out the door and blow a couple of us right out of the saddle. Don't take no skill or even a lot of guts. Best thing we can do is get the money and get out of Candelaria without a shot being fired. Is that understood?"

The brothers nodded their heads, except for Jud, who seemed to be in a disagreeable mood, because he growled, "As long as nobody gets smart or tries to mess with me, I'll let 'em alone. But if someone in that Wells Fargo office tries to stop me, I'll—"

Mitch reached out and grabbed his youngest brother by the shirt front. "Listen, you snot-nosed little peacock! You do as I say in there, and you don't make a damn sound! Is that understood?"

"Let go of me!" Jud struggled until his oldest brother unhanded him, then he screeched, "One of these days I'm gonna have to put a bullet through your damn guts."

"Shut up," Ulysses warned. "Mitch is right. No gunfire. Now let's quit fightin' among ourselves and get the job done."

Jud's eyes were burning with hatred for his oldest brother. When the job was over, maybe he'd see just how fast Mitch still was with a gun. Hell, Ulysses or Hank wouldn't interfere—not when they realized that they'd be cutting up the Candelaria take three ways instead of four.

Jud dismounted and tied his horse. He checked his gun and looked the town over, wondering if anyone had already guessed their purpose for galloping into Candelaria on a scorching day like this.

But the town looked quiet, and nobody appeared to be paying them a damn bit of attention. Well, Jud thought, after today, they'd sure be noticed wherever they rode. And after today, they'd be rich as kings. Rich enough to drink the best whiskey and have the prettiest women—both as often as they wanted.

"All right," Mitch said, splitting off with Hank. "Let's

just pick this town clean and ride away without a shot being fired."

Everyone nodded, except for Jud, who was grinning with anticipation. He had an itchy trigger finger and an urge to be famous. So if trouble came, he'd just show his bothers and everyone else in this two-bit town that he was a man to be reckoned with, by gawd.

TWO

Jud watched Mitch and Hank head toward the bank, for a moment before he turned and followed Ulysses into the Wells Fargo office. It was almost empty except for the manager, who was doubling as a ticket clerk, and a driver who had nothing better to do with his spare time than hang around the company office.

Ulysses smiled and said in a nice, friendly way, "Me and my brother would like to buy a couple of tickets on the next stage to Carson City."

"The next stage leaves at two o'clock," the young manager said. "Fare is eight dollars."

"Each?"

"That's right. It's nearly a hundred miles, you know."

"Seems a little high," Ulysses said, glancing at Jud, who had edged toward the back of the room so that he'd be in a good position to cover the front door as well as the driver.

7

The manager was in a bad mood. His regular ticket clerk had quit the day before and, until Wells Fargo sent him a replacement, he was stuck doing an underling's job, which was a blow to his pride. Even worse, being forced to sell tickets was a great source of embarrassment for his gossipy wife, who had boasted to anyone who would listen that her husband was someday going to be a partner in the great shipping and banking company.

"Mister," the young manager snapped, "I don't establish the fare. I'm not even supposed to be selling tickets. I'm just filling in for an underling. Now, it'll cost sixteen dollars for you and your brother to ride to Carson City."

"All right," Ulysses said, eying the big safe, where he knew the mining payroll was resting. Ulysses pulled out a sack of tobacco and laid it down on the counter. "But all I've got is this big poke of gold dust."

"Take it over to the bank and bring back some currency," the manager said. "I don't accept gold dust."

Ulysses had hoped that the officious young man might voluntarily open the safe and trade him some currency, but his attempt at a ruse had failed. "Well, in that case, I got a confession to make. This ain't gold, it's just my chewin' tobacco in here. Funny, huh?"

"Not a damn bit, mister. Now either fork up the sixteen dollars, or get out of here and stop wasting my time and the company's money."

Ulysses stepped back and casually drew the sixgun on his hip. 'I don't like smart asses," he said, pointing the gun at the man's face. "So open up that safe or say your prayers."

The driver, though unarmed, jumped to his feet and started to lunge at Ulysses, but Jud drew his gun and pistol-whipped the man to the floor.

"I think you'd better open the safe," Jud said to the

manager as the driver twitched at his feet. "And I think you'd better do it real fast."

"Yes, sir!" the manager said, throwing up his hands.

Ulysses moved around behind the counter and shoved his gun into the manager's back. "Lower your hands and work the combination lock."

"There's nothing in here worth dying for," the badly shaken manager said. "Probably not more than two hundred dollars."

"What the hell do you mean?"

"Just what I said."

"The mine payroll is supposed to be going out today!"

"Not until this afternoon. Mister, we don't get it until noon!"

Ulysses glanced up at the clock on the wall. It was eleven o'clock, straight up. Jeezus! They'd have to wait better than an hour just to get their hands on that big mining payroll. He jammed the barrel of his gun into the man's back so hard that the manager grunted with pain and wheezed, "Please don't kill me. I got a wife and—"

"Shut up and open the damn safe before I blow your head off!"

The manager was so rattled he had to try the combination three times before he finally got the safe open. When he did, Ulysses grabbed him by the shoulder and hurled him back against the counter so hard that the man struck his head and was momentarily dazed.

Ulysses reached into the safe and yanked out the contents. Jud came over to the counter and peered over the top to watch. "Was he lyin'? If he was, I'm going to cut his damned throat!"

Ulysses tore open all the sacks and pulled out a handfull of bills, which he thumbed through rapidly. "Dammit, he *wasn't* lying! There ain't but a couple hundred dollars here!"

Jud swore softly. He heard a sound behind him and turned just in time to see the pistol-whipped driver crawling to his hands and knees. Jud stepped back and drove the toe of his boot into the side of the man's head, just below the ear. The driver grunted and dropped facefirst onto the floor.

"What are we going to do now?" Jud asked.

Ulysses stood up and crammed the money into his pants. "Go to the front window. If anyone comes in here, step behind them and use that pistol on their heads. As long as Mitch and Hank are still inside the bank, we gotta stay here and wait anyway. Maybe something is going wrong for them, too. Maybe we can afford to wait another hour for the mining payroll to arrive."

"That's a damn long time," Jud said, not liking the idea a bit. "There's bound to be a lot of folks come in here between now and then, and there'll be a few guards with the payroll. I say we clear out."

"And I say we wait!" Ulysses shouted. "Now get up to that window and keep an eye out for trouble."

Jud went to the front window and peered across the street. "They drew the bank's window shades. Even the one on the door. I can't see a thing that's going on."

"Just keep an eye open and relax. Mitch said the most important thing we could do was just to keep our heads and not use our guns. That's what we're going to do."

At the mention of his oldest brother's name, Jud's anger flared. "I get almighty sick of followin' Mitch's orders. Sick to the death of it, as a matter of fact."

"Then follow my damn orders," Ulysses growled. "'Cause I'm telling you exactly the same damn thing."

Jud buttoned his lip and turned back to watch the street. If they got a big haul this time, he was going to strike out on his own. He was tired of being the youngest and always sucking hind tit. Tired of having to obey Mitch and Ulysses. He was tired of this whole damn way of living.

The minutes crawled by, and finally Jud said, "Here they come!"

Ulysses was furious. "They were supposed to signal and wait for us to come out, too! Dammit, Mitch won't even follow his own plan! Are their saddlebags full?"

"Full to bulging!" Jud sang out.

Ulysses glanced up at the clock again. Only a few minutes had passed, but he said, "If Mitch got his, we're staying right here until noon and getting ours."

"But they're waiting for us!"

Ulysses stomped up to the front window. He pulled back the curtain and waved at Mitch to go on, but his older brother shook his head and began to gesture to him and Jud to hurry outside and join up.

"What are we going to do?" Jud said, suddenly panicked.

"We're going to stay right here," Ulysses said, going stubborn. "If Mitch wants to ride that bad, let him and Hank go. We can catch up with them later. Right now, we're staying."

"Here he comes!" Jud said. "And he looks madder than a teased rattlesnake."

They both watched Mitch come stomping down the street. He'd left Hank to tie the bulging saddlebags on their horses and keep guard. When he rushed inside the Wells Fargo office, he slammed the door behind him and took one look at the unconscious driver and the dazed office manager before he shouted, "What the hell is wrong in here?"

Ulysses told him in a few short words.

"The hell with waiting!" Mitch swore. "By noon, the whole damn town will know we're in here, and they'll cut us to pieces when we try to escape. Come on, we're leaving before someone enters the bank and discovers it's been robbed."

Ulysses folded his thick arms across his chest. "You said the mine payroll is worth five, maybe even ten thousand dollars."

"Sure I said that, but no amount of money is worth dying for! Now let's get the hell out of this town before the lid flies off and we have to shoot our way out of Candelaria!"

"How much did you get you get at the bank?" Jud asked.

"How should I know?" Mitch was practically screaming at him. "You think I've got time to count the money?"

"You must have stuffed the saddlebags and got some damned idea," Ulysses said. "How much?"

Mitch swore in exasperation. "All right. Ten or twelve thousand, easy. Now are you satisfied? Can we get out of here?"

Ulysses nodded, and so did Jud. Three thousand dollars each was enough money to take a man a long way in this country.

"Just a minute," Jud said, pulling his knife. "That manager will stand up and start screaming as soon as we walk out the door."

Mitch hurried around the counter to catch the manager, who was trying to squeeze under the counter and hide. Mitch grabbed the terrified man by the belt and yanked him out, then cocked his gun.

The manager clasped his hands together in supplication. "Please, don't kill me! I've got a wife and—"

Mitch pistol-whipped the man and turned toward the door. Ulysses and Jud were already crossing the street to the horses, and big Hank was mounted and ready to ride.

Mitch didn't want to attract attention, so he didn't run,

but he sure walked fast. He kept staring at the bank, and just as he was about to take his reins and shove his foot in the stirrups, a man staggered out of the bank and began to yell, "The bank's been robbed! The bank's been robbed!"

"Shit!" Mitch swore, jamming his boot into his stirrup and swinging onto his horse as someone opened fire from the saloon.

A bullet cut across the street, and the Pike brothers heard its angry thump when it struck the hitching rail and splintered wood.

"Let's get out of here!" Mitch shouted.

They spurred their horses down the street as the men of Candelaria began to open fire from their store fronts. Bullets were buzzing as thick and angry as hornets, but the brothers kept their heads down low and their own guns working. Ulysses, being the best man among them with a gun, killed two men before they reached the end of town, and young Jud drilled another.

"Yippeee!" Jud screamed as they spurred back down the stage road.

"Look!" Mitch shouted. "That rider we passed on the black horse is heading straight at us."

The Gunsmith *was* coming. He had heard the gun battle, and when the Pike brothers had suddenly come charging out of Candelaria, it did not take a whole hell of a lot of brains to add up the score and realize what was happening. Most men would have reined their horses off the road and ridden like blazes to get out of shooting range of the four Pike brothers.

But Clint Adams wasn't like most men. He was the Gunsmith, and he was accustomed to being up against bad odds. So instead of running, he'd drawn his gun and touched his spurs to the black gelding's flanks.

"He must be crazy!" Jud shouted, spurring into the lead. "I'm gonna drill him dead center."

Jud began firing too early, and Clint waited until the distance was reasonable before he cooly aimed and shot the youngest Pike brother through the chest. Jud screamed, then flipped over the back of his racing horse. His brothers opened fire, and Clint managed to wing big Hank in the shoulder before his own horse suddenly collapsed under him when a bullet creased its neck.

Clint kicked out of his stirrups and sailed headfirst into the brush. His main concern was for his horse, but when the three remaining Pike brothers came after him, he let them know that he would not sell his life cheaply. And when he also winged Mitch, the brothers broke off the attack and went racing south toward the California border.

Clint staggered to his feet and hobbled over to his fallen horse. Duke had not taken a fatal bullet. But the big gelding was definitely in need of a veterinarian's attention. The neck crease was deep and bleeding heavily.

Clint glanced over at Jud Pike, who lay dead on the hard, rocky road. "They were your brothers, weren't they?" he said between clenched teeth. "I'm sure you're already knocking on the gates of hell. And I promise you this, before I'm through, you're going to be joined by every damn one of your brothers!"

Clint watched the three riders disappear over a brush-covered hill. He turned his attention back to his horse, knowing he had to urge the gelding to its feet.

"You won't last very long out here on the ground," he said.

The black horse groaned, and then it threw its two front legs out like a pair of hayhooks and pulled its weight up. The horse stood unsteadily as Clint patted its muscular neck. "Candelaria isn't but another mile up this road," he said. "I'm going to find you a veterinarian, some grain, and cool water. I promise I'll make things up to you. Now come along."

Duke shook his head and followed the Gunsmith into Candelaria.

THREE

Clint led Duke into Candelaria, expecting to see a sheriff and a posse come busting out of town at any moment, hot on the heels of the three bank robbers. But by the time he finally reached town, he realized that there wasn't going to be any pursuit. And when he entered the main street, he saw a lot of grim-faced miners and townspeople standing around four bodies.

What the hell was going on here? Why wasn't a posse being formed? Clint curbed his disgust and knew that his first duty was to his wounded horse. "Is there a veterinarian in this town?" Clint shouted at the silent throng.

One man finally turned and said, "Ain't no veterinarian in Candelaria. Doc Huthman takes care of the sick animals and pulls bad teeth. But the doc is taking care of Mr. Eubanks, the Wells Fargo manager, along with several other people who got hurt. Hell, we got four dead men, here, mister! Nobody's gonna get too excited about a shot horse."

Clint bristled. "You got *five* dead men, including the one I killed out on the road south of town."

Now people turned away from their morbid fascination with the corpses and stared at the Gunsmith.

One, a big fella with his sleeves rolled up around his thick forearms, said, "I'm Heck Jacobs, the blacksmith. I got some salve and if you shot one of the Pike brothers, I'd be honored to doctor and board your horse for free at my stable."

Clint relaxed a little. "I accept your offer. But why in the deuce are all you folks just standing around? Why isn't your sheriff getting a posse formed and going after those three? Hell, I wounded two of 'em."

"You did!" A short, bald man in a dark suit detached himself from the others and said, "I'm Roy Perkins. I own the general store, and I'm the mayor of this town. Now, you say that you killed one of the Pike brothers and wounded two more? Frankly, I find that unbelievable."

"Well, I find the fact that you folks are content just to stand around while those men make good their escape is also pretty damned unbelievable."

"Say," a tall man in a bartender's apron yelled, stepping forward to point at Clint. "I seen you before. Seen you in a gunfight over in Abilene about three years ago. Aren't you the man they call the Gunsmith?"

Clint scowled. He did not particularly like that moniker, or the instant and considerable attention it always generated. And yet, the Gunsmith was a name he could not shake. It might cause him more grief than not, especially when young fools seeking a quick reputation tried to brace him, but it was the name he had to live with all the same.

"I've been called that," he admitted. "But right now, what I need is doctoring for my horse."

The blacksmith came forward. He stuck out a big hand that was as dry and brittle as the bark on a pine tree, and then he nearly crushed Clint's fist when he said, "One of those boys stretched out dead is my cousin. If you killed one of the Pike brothers and wounded two others, you're a hero to me, Gunsmith. Here. Let me take care of your horse."

"Thank you," Clint said, as the people of Candelaria stared at him with the same fixed curiosity they'd just shown the corpses.

Clint scowled. "Those three men must be five miles away at least. Did they get any money?"

"Cleaned out my bank," a small, gray-haired man in a brown suit said. "I expect they got nearly fifteen thousand dollars in cash. Would have gotten a whole lot more at the Wells Fargo office if they'd waited another hour."

"Then why isn't this town and its sheriff riding the hell after them?"

The banker took a sudden interest in the toes of his polished shoes.

"Well?"

Mayor Perkins cleared his throat. "You understand. The last sheriff we had was gunned down by Ulysses Pike. And you see, the Pike brothers knew all of us. Hell, they've gambled and hoo-rawed this town dozens of times. Mostly they just get drunk, and people sort of steer wide of them. Except when the sheriff made the foolish mistake of trying to jail all four of them, they never did no big wrong."

Clint removed his hat and sleeved the sweat from his brow. "They shot the sheriff who was trying to arrest them, and you say they never did no 'big wrong'? Mister Mayor, if you don't think gunning down your sheriff is wrong, what the devil is?"

In answer, Roy Perkins turned and pointed to the four dead men. "That's what I consider a *real* wrong," he said in a grave voice. "And taking our money is wrong. But at the same time, we're town people. Merchants and miners. We'll fight if and when we have to, but we're not gunmen, as you can plainly see by the body count we have here. Why, we were all shooting at them, and not a darned one of us hit a Pike. But four of our own are dead."

"If that's what really happened, then the Pike brothers were mighty lucky," Clint said. "And those four men that died will have died for nothing if you don't go after them."

A woman's voice cut across the street from the second story of the Candelaria Hotel. "They won't go," she said with scorn. "Except for the ones that died and maybe a couple others, what you're facing is a bunch of damned rabbits."

Clint turned, along with the others, to see a tall, buxom blonde.

"Never mind her," the mayor whispered. "She's poor Sheriff Malloy's widow, and when he was gunned down, she went a little teched."

Clint said nothing. The woman might be 'teched' but she was sure a looker. Mrs. Malloy had an hour-glass figure and a very angry, but pretty face. She might have been twenty-five, but not a day older, and it made the Gunsmith feel even sorrier for the poor sheriff who would die for the likes of these do-nothing townspeople.

"Now, Mrs. Malloy," the mayor said, "in this time of great sorrow, we don't need that kind of hard talk."

"Sure you do!" She lifted her chin. "You men are just plain afraid of the Pike brothers, and you always have been. The four dead are the only ones in this town who deserve to wear pants!"

"I resent that!" the mayor cried. "Just because we aren't gunfighters doesn't—"

"You're a bunch of mice, is what you are," the widow spat. "When Ulysses Pike shot down my husband, you didn't lift a hand, even though my husband took your damn badge on your promise that he'd have help when it was needed. That help never came, and it never will from the spineless likes of this town."

The miners and other men stirred restlessly, and there was a good deal of angry muttering, but no one challenged the woman until after she turned and disappeared back into the hotel. Then everyone seemed to open up and bitterly denounce her cutting accusations.

Clint just shook his head and gave up on the bunch of them. He had no use for a bunch of townsfolk who would allow four of their own to be killed and then would do nothing about it. No use at all.

He walked up to Heck Jacobs' big and prosperous-looking stable and found the blacksmith had already unsaddled Duke and was rubbing a salve into the crease across the top of the gelding's thick neck. Clint sidled up to the horse and said, "How is he doing?"

"He's fine," the blacksmith said. "If the bullet had been an inch lower, he'd be dogmeat. But he's a hell of a fine animal, and I can see why you're pretty upset."

Clint scratched behind the black gelding's ears. "We've been through a lot together, and this horse has saved my bacon more than once. Out there on the road when I shot the one brother dead, I swore I'd get even with the others. But after hearing and watching your mayor and those people, I think I lost my appetite for helping recover this town's money and bringing those men to justice. I'm just going to give this horse a day or two of rest, then keep riding north."

"Not that simple," Jacobs said, finding a currycomb and beginning to brush Duke's slick coat.

"What is that supposed to mean?"

"It means that if you really did kill one of them and wound two others, they'll be coming back to kill you. I know all them brothers, and I know how they think. You got a big problem, Gunsmith."

Clint was not sure that he had heard correctly. "Do you mean that they'd actually be bold enough to come right into Candelaria and exact their revenge?"

"Not in broad daylight. Despite what the sheriff's widow said, there's a few men in this town who qualify for wearing pants. I'm one, and there are others who would try and shoot the Pikes on sight. But those brothers are mean, and they hold a grudge. One thing sure, they can't allow you to do what you did to them out on the road and get away with it. They do that, folks will get the notion that they can all be killed."

Clint found another currycomb and began to brush his side of the gelding as he chewed on the blacksmith's words. He finished brushing and said, "Jacobs, did you lose any money in that bank they robbed?"

"My life's savings," the blacksmith replied. "Almost a thousand dollars."

"And you're just going to let it go without a fight?"

The big blacksmith showed a spark of anger for the first time. "Listen! I said I'd be one of the few who'd shoot the Pikes on sight. I reckon I meant what I said, even though I'm not that damn good with a gun, and there ain't one chance in a hundred that I'd live through a gunfight against any of the Pike brothers. They're all good, but Ulysses, now he's so fast he's almost inhuman. Everyone who's been in Candelaria more than a few months saw him outdraw and riddle Sheriff Malloy. And Malloy was fast! But Ulysses Pike emptied his gun before the sheriff could even clear leather."

Clint took a deep breath and let it out slowly. "So what's

his wife still doing in a place that wouldn't even back her husband up?"

"She and the sheriff owned the Candelaria Hotel. Everyone expected her to sell it and move on after her husband's death, but she stayed, and she's like salt rubbing in a wound that won't heal. She speaks out, shaming the townspeople every chance she gets. Maybe she is teched. I don't know. She was fine before her husband was gunned down."

"What about you?" Clint said, "Did you just let it happen without raising a hand?"

Heck Jacobs was big and strong and, when angered, his dark eyes sparked like flint. "I tried to help. I didn't have a gun, so I grabbed up the spoke of a wheel and went after them. But that giant, Hank Pike, he tackled me from behind and sledged me behind the ear. I couldn't get him off my back, and he just beat the livin' hell out of me. When I woke up, the Pike brothers were gone, and the sheriff was full of bullet holes."

"Then you've got nothing to be ashamed about," Clint said, "except for staying in a town full of blowhards."

"They aren't all blowhards. If they were, four good men including my cousin wouldn't be laid out for the mortician."

"You're right," Clint said. "I'm sorry. It's just that I've been the sheriff of a good many towns myself, and I never came across one like this. From the looks of things, this town is booming."

"That's a fact. We've got nearly a thousand people living here. As long as the Northern Belle and the other mines keep people working, my business is gonna grow and prosper."

"A town without guts or a conscience has no future," Clint said.

"Well spoken!"

The Gunsmith turned to see the tall, blonde widow standing in the doorway. Clint removed his hat and said, "I heard about your husband and the circumstances of his death. As a man who's been sheriff of more than a few towns, I offer my sympathies."

"Thank you," the woman said, coming inside the barn. She smiled at Heck Jacobs and said, "Heck, I came because I wanted you to know that I lost my temper, and I was wrong when I said there were no men fit to wear pants in Candelaria. You're a brave man, and there are few others. I just wanted you to know that you weren't included among the 'mice' that I was referring to."

The powerful blacksmith ran his dirty hands down the front of his shirt as if to smooth it, and he nodded. "I knew you didn't include me, Molly. This here is Clint Adams, better known at the Gunsmith."

The woman came up and shook Clint's hand firmly. She was just as pretty close as she was from a distance, but her smile was sad. "I just heard that someone managed to build up enough courage to ride south, where they found Jud Pike with a bullet through his heart. I want to thank you for killing him. I just wish it had been Ulysses."

"I understand," Clint said.

She looked deep into his eyes. "Yes, I am sure you do. Will you also understand when I make you a proposition?"

"Proposition? What kind?"

"I own the Candelaria Hotel, and it has a value of at least three thousand dollars," she said. "If you will track down and kill the Pike brothers, it is yours, free and clear."

While Clint closed his jaw, Molly Malloy looked to the blacksmith. "Heck," she said, "you're the only man I trust enough to hold an agreement that will state the offer that I have just made. Will you do it?"

"Sure, Molly, but—"

"Just do it, please," she said, turning back to Clint.

"Mr. Adams, will you accept my offer? Before you answer, I should also tell you that I do not care if you bring back the thousands of dollars stolen from our bank or not. If you want, keep it."

"I couldn't do that." Clint frowned. "And I couldn't take your hotel for doing what seems should have already been done by a posse."

The woman's shoulders sagged a little, and the confidence he had seen only moments ago drained away. "Please," she whispered. "I can't leave Candelaria before my husband's death is vindicated by the death of those terrible men. I've suffered from the Pike brothers for years and years."

When Clint's't eyebrows raised, she took a deep breath and said, "My late husband was the only one who knew that I had been raped by the Pike brothers when I was just fourteen. They did it many times after that, and I was powerless to stop them. My father was afraid of them, and my mother was dead. It wasn't until I was able to buy a gun—"

Clint reached out to the woman and instinctively drew her to his chest. He felt her shake, and he whispered into her blonde hair, "You don't have to say another thing, Mrs. Malloy. I'll go after them, and I'll bring them to justice. But I won't take your hotel for doing what is right."

"I'm coming, too," the blacksmith said in a voice that shook with fury.

Clint started to object, because a man like Heck Jacobs was often more of a danger than a help in this kind of work. But when he saw the pain and anger in Jacobs' square face, he knew that the blacksmith was secretly in love with Molly Malloy, and no words on Earth could have made him remain in Candelaria as long as the Pike brothers were alive and free.

"All right," Clint said. "I'll leave in a couple of days, when my horse has had a chance to recover."

Molly Malloy pulled out of Clint's arms. "But I thought you'd want to get right on their trail!"

"From what Heck tells me, the Pike brothers aren't going to run very far. In fact, he predicts that they'll be coming for me."

"That's true," the blacksmith said. "Molly, you know how their minds work. They won't be able to stomach losing young Jud. He was the baby of the family, and they'll want to take their revenge."

Molly's pretty face was suddenly marred with bitterness. "Jud was no baby. What he was I can't tell you. Animal is too kind a word to describe him. I'm glad he's dead!"

Clint and the blacksmith exchanged glances and then looked away. They could only guess at what Jud must have done to Molly to make her so hate-filled at the mention of his name.

After a moment, Molly seemed to get a grip on herself. She whispered, "I'm sorry. When it comes to those . . . those horrible men, I almost go crazy. I've been hating them for so long, I guess I'm half-poisoned. And when they shot my husband to death right here on the main street of town and nobody except Heck tried to help him—well . . . I nearly lost my mind."

"Molly," Clint said. "I've killed a few outlaws, and I've comforted a few widows in my career. Besides that, you might be able to tell me a few things about the Pikes that will save our lives. Why don't we have dinner together?"

She lifted her head and forced a grateful smile. "I'd like that very much. Come by my hotel at eight o'clock. Heck, would you—?"

"No," the blacksmith said, too quickly. "You and the Gunsmith get acquainted. I've got to find a man to watch over my livery before we go after the Pike brothers. I've got plenty to do between now and then, and if I don't see you before we ride, then you take care. If anything happens to me, this place is yours."

Molly's face softened. "Oh, Heck! Don't even say that!"

Clint took his currycomb up again and began to work on Duke's tail, and he did not look up from the brushing until Molly Malloy was gone.

FOUR

It had been a pleasant dinner, and now that they were through eating, Clint leaned back in his chair and considered the widow Malloy with considerable interest. "You have a very nice hotel here, and your chef is to be congratulated."

"Thank you," Molly said. "Actually, he's an old cowboy cook, but he's one of the best. He arrived in Candelaria for the same reason they all do—to strike it rich—but he injured his hand in a mining accident. I hired him the next day, and I've never regretted it."

"I get the impression that you are a very decisive woman," Clint said. "You make decisions in a hurry, and I'll bet that you stand by them."

"I do," Molly said. "Sometimes it gets me into trouble. For example, I judge men almost from the moment I first see them. I consider myself rather intuitive, and I've rarely made mistakes when it comes to judging a man's character, or lack of character."

Clint was amused. "All right. Am I or am I not a gentleman?"

"You are," Molly said. "Not in the strict sense of the word, but in the ways that count. I sense in you a strong bit of chivalry, honest, a healthy dash of pride, and, above all, you're a very honorable man."

"You say that even knowing that I'm called the Gunsmith?"

"That's just a name. I can look into your eyes and see that you're a man of great integrity and determination."

"And I," Clint said, "can look into your eyes and see that you are very good at the blarney."

The woman laughed, and her voice was as light and gay as the tinkle of a bell. "I should have known that flattery would get me nowhere."

'That's not true, Molly."

Her smile faded. "What I said about you might have been flattering, but it was my true assessment. I think you are the man who can right a great wrong. You're the only man who has any chance at all of either killing or capturing the Pike brothers."

"Is that all you really care about?"

"Yes. I told you that Ulysses gunned down my husband and that all the Pike brothers raped me when I was barely coming into womanhood. Can you blame me for wanting them dead?"

"No," Clint said. "But it seems as though it's become something of an obsession with you. You're even willing to hand this entire hotel over to me if I kill the Pike brothers."

"I can always make good money," Molly said, avoiding his eyes. "Enough money to eventually buy another hotel, if that was what I wanted most. But I can't buy back my virginity or the years of terror that those men caused me.

Or the nights I spent waiting for them to come, when I was sick with dread. Or the way my father looked after they came in the night and rode away in the morning, and he did nothing to stop them.

"Most of all," Molly said in a voice that shook with bitterness, "I can't buy back my husband, who was gunned down in cold blood by a man whom he knew he couldn't outdraw. Clint, there are a few facts that you'd better know about the Pike brothers."

"Anything you can say will be helpful."

"Ulysses is the one who is the fastest."

"Which is he?"

"He's the one with a scar down the right side of his face. I hear he got it in a knife fight down in Mexico. I don't know about that. He's the quietest of the three, and the most dangerous. My husband said that he was inhumanly fast."

"He'd be the only one I didn't wing when they charged past me heading south. What about the giant?"

"He's slow, but he likes to inflict pain. If he gets his hands on an enemy, he's strong enough to tear them limb from limb. He's not a bit clever, but I guess you'd say he'd be the last one you'd want to meet in a dark cave."

"And the third man?"

"He's their leader. His name is Mitch. I used to think he had a streak of decency in him, but I was wrong. When I was a little girl, he was the first one to take advantage of me. He was never cruel, but he is very smart. If the others would listen to him, they'd be better off. But Jud always hated his oldest brother, and I think Ulysses is jealous of Mitch. Just watch out for him. He isn't so fast or strong, but he always seems to find a way to win. He seems unbeatable."

"I'll watch out for him," Clint promised. "Although

from what you've told me, all three sound plenty dangerous."

"They are. And the one you killed, Jud, he was the only fool among them. He had a temper that was uncontrollable. Whenever he got mad, I thought he was going to kill me. But he never did, and I am so glad that he's dead."

"So am I," Clint said, looking closely at the woman. He could not be sure, but he thought that she might even have been in love with Jud at some point in her youth. There was just something about the way she hated the man so intensely that said he'd been the one who'd hurt her most of all.

Clint leaned closer to the woman. "I just wish there was some way besides killing the Pike brothers or bringing them to the hangman for me to help ease the pain of your loss."

"There is," she told him.

Somehow, the way she said it, and the way she looked at him told Clint everything he needed to know. Without a word, he took her arm, and they left the dining room. They walked upstairs to the hotel room, where she now lived alone, and the moment they were inside and alone, Molly was in his arms, her lips soft and yet very insistent.

Clint picked the woman up and carried her to the large, four-poster bed. He placed her down on the pink chiffon spread and slowly undressed her until she wore nothing but a look of anticipation.

"Hurry up and undress," she breathed, her eyes burning with desire.

"All right, but I could stand here and admire you half the night."

Clint unbuckled his gun belt and hung it on the bedpost. He unbuttoned his shirt and shrugged out of it before he sat down on the edge of the bed and pulled off his boots and socks.

"You have a few scars of your own," Molly said, touching his side, where an old bullet wound had left the flesh puckered.

Clint stood up and removed his pants and underclothing before he sat down next to the woman, and his hands cupped her breasts. "I healed just fine, and you will, too, if you give yourself a chance."

In reply, Molly reached down, and her hands found his manhood, then began to massage it lovingly. Clint felt himself grow long and stiff with anticipation. "You're a beautiful woman."

She gently pushed him back on the bed, then slid down his body, her tongue making wet circles on his chest, then his hard stomach, and finally, the insides of his thighs. Clint groaned and ran his fingers through her thick, blonde hair. He pulled her onto him, and when her mouth envolped his throbbing manhood, he expelled a deep breath and let her do what she wanted.

Molly wanted all of him. Her lips and her tongue moved up and down his long shaft, making it throb and then ache with the need for release. Clint could not stop his hips from moving up and down and she worked him so skillfully that he knew she was very experienced. He wondered if the Pike brothers had made her learn to do this, but he dismissed the thought as she groaned with pleasure and then finally slid back onto the bed.

Clint rolled over onto her and felt her hands taking his wet root and fitting it between her legs. When he looked into her face, he saw that she was burning with desire. Her eyes flashed, and her lips were pulled back from her teeth. He lowered his mouth to her breasts, and when he sucked one of her hard nipples, she moaned and squirmed. "Please, don't make me wait. I haven't had a man for too long now."

Clint reached down, grabbed two handfuls of her round

buttocks and drove his big rod deep inside her. She cried out with pleasure and arched her back. He pushed his penis in to the hilt, and then he began to slam his body in and out of her, because it was obvious that she was the kind of woman who enjoyed it rough. Later, he'd tantalize her until she begged for more, but right now, they were both too hungry for each other to use finesse.

"Oh, yes!" she cried as his body moved faster and faster. Molly locked her legs behind the small of his back, and her own hands found his buttocks as she pulled him in as far as he could go. Her womanhood milked him furiously, and when she nipped his shoulder and cried out with ecstasy, Clint felt her insides fasten on him like a fist.

"Come on, baby!" he breathed. "Come now!"

Molly exploded like a volcano blowing its top. She began to buck like a wild filly, and her legs flew out straight and flapped uncontrollably as he filled her with his seed.

"Don't stop!" she cried. "Don't ever stop!"

Clint growled like a lion as his body worked like a piston.

Later, he held Molly tight, and she told him that the Pike brothers had a place down in the California desert that they used to hole up in. Jud had once told her all about a rock house and an oasis in a terrible part of the desert called Death Valley. It was there that the brothers had always believed that they could go without being chased, for no posse in its right mind would follow them through the burning desert sands.

"Did he say anything more about this Death Valley?"

"Yes," Molly said. "When we were both just kids, the first time he took me was after promising he'd take me there and feed me to the sidewinders and the scorpions if I didn't pleasure him the way he wanted."

"He's dead," Clint said. "And if they come after me or they run—either way—I'll win. I swear that I will."

She nuzzled his chest. "Try not to let Heck Jacobs get killed. He'll make a pretty big target."

"I know that. He's in love with you, Molly."

"Of course he is," she said. "He's been in love with me since we were kids."

"But you don't feel that way about him?"

"No," Molly said. "He's a fine man, but he smells like a barnyard. I think he's still a virgin, too. And he's so big. You know, Hank Pike used to almost split me in half. He's huge, and he'd force himself into me until I'd scream, thinking I was being impaled by a fence post. Really big, muscular men like him scare me to death, Clint."

The Gunsmith didn't know what to say. He'd caught a glimpse of Hank Pike, and the man was a gorilla. A man who would rape and abuse a girl deserved to be castrated before he was hung.

Clint kissed Molly. "Heck Jacobs might need to bathe more often, but he's a good man, Molly. He'd be gentle and tender."

Molly reached down and took Clint's limp manhood and began to massage it into stiffness. "I've got the man I want right in my hand. So why don't you stop talking and show me a little action?"

Clint laughed and then he happily obliged the woman.

FIVE

Clint awoke the next morning to the sound of loud knocking on Molly's door. The woman beside him stirred but did not awaken. Clint slipped out of bed and pulled his pants on. "Who is it?" he whispered through the crack in the door.

"Is that you, Gunsmith?"

"Yeah. What do you want?"

"My name is Ernie Eubanks, and I need to talk to you."

"It can wait."

"No, it can't," Eubanks said. "I'm the manager of the Wells Fargo office, and I need to see you right away."

Clint sighed. "I'll meet you at your office as soon as I get dressed. Now get the hell out of here."

"Thanks," Eubanks said.

Clint heard the man's footsteps recede down the hallway. Clint went over to the bed, sat down, and started to

34

get dressed. Molly rolled over and knuckled the sleep from her eyes.

"What did he want at this hour?"

"Damned if I know," Clint said.

Molly pushed herself up on one elbow. "My guess is that his wife, Ruth, is after him to do something about the robbery."

"I didn't even know that Wells Fargo was robbed yesterday."

"I don't think it was for much," Molly said. "But they've got a policy that, no matter how much they lose in a theft, they'll offer a reward."

"Good," Clint said. "I can use the extra money."

Molly watched him finish dressing and then buckle on his gun belt. "When will you leave?"

"As soon as I'm sure my horse is all right."

"Wouldn't you rather wait for the Pikes to come back here?"

"No," Clint said. "For one thing, two of those brothers are wounded. Not bad, but enough that they'll be in some pain. This is the time to get them. Not later, when they chose the time and place."

Clint reached for his black Stetson. "You got any idea where they might run?"

"Death Valley," Molly said without hesitation.

"Damn," Clint muttered. "That's just about the last place on Earth that I want to go trailing after them. And right in the middle of summer, when there is a killing heat."

Molly reached for him. "Then you should wait. They'll show up sooner or later."

Clint kissed her lips and then one of her lush breasts, but before she could fully distract him, he made himself leave. "I'd better talk to Eubanks. It sounds like he's in sort of a hurry."

"Come right back," Molly said, "I'll be here waiting."

"I'll do that," the Gunsmith promised, letting himself out the door.

When he entered the Wells Fargo office a few minutes later, he walked right into a raging argument between Eubanks and a pretty but sharp-tongued woman, who was giving the man hell.

"You *have* to do it!" she was saying. "Ernie, if you ever want to be made an executive of Wells Fargo, then—"

"Excuse me," Clint said, removing his hat. "Maybe I should come back later."

"No," Eubanks said. "My wife was just about to leave, weren't you, dear?"

But Ruth Eubanks had other plans. Her eyes surveyed the Gunsmith from head to toe, and she smiled and extended her hand. "So, at last I meet the famous Gunsmith. My, you certainly did arrive at the right moment."

"What do you mean?"

Ruth fluttered her eyelashes. She was tall, well endowed, and had beautiful brown hair that fell in soft curls almost to her waist. "Well," she said, "you did kill Jud and wound two of the others. What a courageous act!"

The woman was looking at him so boldly that Clint was glad that her husband could not see the open invitation in Ruth Eubanks' brown eyes. She licked her lips with the tip of her tongue and added, "I've never met a legend before, Mr. Gunsmith."

"Adams," he said, wishing she would leave before her husband realized that she was acting so suggestively. "It's Clint Adams, and I had better talk to your husband now."

Ruth nodded, then turned to her husband. "He wants to go with you and help capture the Pike brothers, don't you, Ernie?"

The young Wells Fargo manager nodded his head with more than a little reluctance. "That's right."

"I don't think that's such a good idea," Clint said, trying to be diplomatic. "Mrs. Malloy tells me that they've probably ridden into Death Valley. I don't know if you've ever been there, but I have. It's a—excuse my language, Mrs. Eubanks—but it's hell on Earth."

She smiled. "I don't mind cussing of that nature, Mr. Adams. And I'm sure that your description is apt. However, my husband was assaulted and his office robbed. I'm sure you understand that he feels a moral obligation to accompany you and a posse into Death Valley."

"I doubt there'll even be a posse," Clint said. "Heck Jacobs is going with me, but other than him, that's probably the extent of it."

The woman didn't bat an eye or hesitate for an instant, so determined was she that her husband should go to kill or capture the outlaw brothers. "Then all the more reason why you need Ernie. With my husband along, the odds will be even. Without him, it would be three against the two of you."

Clint scowled at the Wells Fargo office manager. The man simply did not look like the kind who could or would endure much hardship. He was slender, nice looking, but soft and a little effeminate to Clint's way of thinking. "Ernie, can you ride a horse?"

"Of course he can!" Ruth interrupted with a tone that left no doubt she thought her husband had been insulted.

Clint was running out of patience. "Mrs. Eubanks, I'm asking your husband. Will you let him answer the questions?"

Stung by his words, Ruth's smile slipped badly. "Of course! Go ahead and answer the man, Ernie."

"Yeah, I can ride a horse."

Clint was not greatly reassured. "What about a gun or a rifle? How good a marksman are you?"

Eubanks glanced at his now stern-faced wife. "Well," he stammered, "I used to shoot sometimes when I was a boy. You know, squirrel-hunting and the like. But during the past ten years or so, well, I'm probably a little rusty."

"You're probably damn rusty," Clint said. "I just don't think it would be a good idea if you came along."

"But he *has* to go along!"

"No, he doesn't," Clint said sternly. "And a man that's not physically and mentally up to Death Valley and a gunfight is just more trouble than he's worth. I mean no offense, Mr. Eubanks, but you'd be just one more worry on my mind if I took you after the Pike brothers."

Eubanks looked relieved, but his wife was furious. "You don't understand. If he goes and helps capture the Pike brothers, it could be our ticket out of Candelaria. My husband would get a big promotion and—"

"Lady," Clint said, trying not to lose his temper completely, "I don't give a damn about his promotion, and neither should you if you understand the risks he'd be taking in a desert manhunt."

Clint looked up at the poor manager. Mrs. Eubanks might be pretty, but she was the kind of scheming woman who drove men into an early grave. "Ernie, if our business is finished, I'll be moseying along. I want to check on my horse and start thinking about getting things together."

"Of course," the manager said, looking thoroughly crestfallen. "I'm sorry to have bothered you this morning."

"Never mind that."

"How is Mrs. Malloy these days?" Ruth asked with raised eyebrows and in a voice that dripped with condemnation.

"She's a lot better than you," Clint snapped as he marched out the door before he got really angry.

He went to see Duke and found that his gelding seemed to have completely recovered. Heck Jacobs had fed him early in the morning and was cleaning the stalls when Clint arrived.

Clint stepped out of the gelding's stall. "Duke looks good."

"He's fine," the blacksmith said without glancing up from his work. "So, when are we going after the Pike brothers?"

"How about this evening, when it cools down?"

"Suits me fine. I've got a man ready to step in and take over."

It suddenly occurred to the Gunsmith that the blacksmith was avoiding his eyes. Clint could guess the reason why. "Heck, I think we'd better have an honest talk before this goes any farther."

The blacksmith finally looked up at him. "What's there to talk about?"

"Mrs. Malloy."

The blacksmith went back to raking manure. "What she does is none of my business."

"That doesn't seem to be the case," Clint said. "You're in love with Molly, and you're angry because you think Molly and I spent the night together. I don't want to ride out on an outlaw trail with a man who's angry at me."

Heck Jacobs looked up, and even in the dim interior of the barn, his eyes blazed with anger. "You did sleep with her, didn't you?"

"Yeah," Clint said, wondering if the blacksmith was going to take a roundhouse swing at him or not. He sure looked angry enough to do it. "Yeah, I slept with her."

Jacobs gritted his teeth so hard that the muscles in his jaw ridged like ropes. "She's a decent woman! You want to screw someone, why don't you find some whore and—"

"Stop it!" Clint barked. "The woman wanted me, and I

wanted her, and that's all there is to the story. Now if you aren't man enough to accept that, then stay the hell here and shovel real manure. I don't need you."

Jacobs gripped the rake he was using until his knuckles grew white. Clint turned on his heel and started to leave, but Jacobs shouted, "All right! You win, dammit! And you're right. It's none of my concern. Molly is a grown woman, and she can make her own choices."

Clint stopped and turned back to face the man. "Molly thinks a great deal of you, but she doesn't love you, Heck. Maybe that will change, but maybe it won't. Don't be coming along with me trying to earn Molly's love. It never works that way. Come because you think it's the right thing for you to do."

Heck Jacobs nodded his big head. "It is the right thing for me to do. I loved my cousin, and he didn't deserve to die yesterday. Molly's late husband was also a friend, and he didn't deserve to die, either. So that's why I'm riding out with you this evening."

"Good," Clint said. "Just keep reminding yourself of that, and we'll get along just fine."

Late that evening, when Clint and the blacksmith were saddled and had their supplies all cinched down on their horses, they mounted up and rode out of Jacobs' barn to find that Ernie Eubanks was waiting for them astride a horse. He was wearing a six-gun on his lean hip, and there was a Winchester repeater in his rifle scabbard. "I'm coming, too," he announced.

"I thought we'd already decided that it would be better for you to stay here and run your Wells Fargo office," Clint said.

"*You* decided; I didn't."

"Go home," Clint said.

"I can't."

"Then find a better wife," Clint said. "One who won't be pushing you so damned hard."

"I love the one I've got. I'm just trying to measure up." Eubanks looked at Clint, then at the blacksmith. "Please let me come along. I can help."

The Gunsmith wanted to bite nails in frustration, but instead he expelled a sigh and said in a voice filled with disgust, "Do you promise that, no matter how tough it gets out there, you won't be bellyaching?"

"I promise."

"Then you can come, but I won't take the responsibility for you—for either of you. I've been a law man too many years to think I can protect you if we ride into a trap or the breaks go against us."

Heck Jacobs said, "Save your breathe."

"All right, then," Clint said. "Let's ride."

They galloped out of Candelaria, passing both Molly Malloy and Ruth Eubanks on the sidewalk. It seemed to Clint that both the men at his side were going on this hunt because of women they loved, but who didn't love them. Those were bad reasons for a man to risk his neck.

In fact, they were about the sorriest reasons in the world.

SIX

Ulysses Pike was pissed. "I tell you, we ought to go back to Candelaria, find that lucky sonofabitch on the black horse, and hang him by his balls!"

Hank Pike agreed. "He killed Jud, gawddammit! Mitch, we can't just let him get away with that!"

"Yeah," Mitch spat, "well, what are we supposed to do? We both got bullet wounds, and neither one of us is in any condition to shoot anybody."

"Speak for yourself," Ulysses said. "I'm the best among us with a gun anyway, and I didn't take no bullet."

"If you're so damned good with a gun, how come that fella is still alive?" Mitch asked.

"Because he got lucky; his horse went down and threw him in the brush, saving his life." Ulysses glared at his older brother, daring him to argue.

Instead, Mitch reined in his horse and stood up wearily in his stirrups. He studied the terrible expanse of desert all around him and figured that whoever had named this Death Valley sure had pegged it right. Mitch reached inside his shirt and felt the scabbed-over wound where one of his ribs had been nicked. His side was stiff and painful, but he knew that he was lucky to be alive.

"I'll tell you what, Ulysses: I don't think the man on the black gelding was any ordinary cowboy. No ordinary fella would have charged the four of us with a smoking gun. No sirree! I think what we ran into was a fella I heard of once before. A fella who rides a black horse and whose description fits that straight-shootin' sonofabitch's to the letter."

"What's his name?"

"The Gunsmith."

"Even *I've* heard of him," Hank said, obviously very impressed. "Gee. You mean I got winged in the arm by someone famous?"

"I think so," Mitch said. "The man who drew us down would be about the Gunsmith's age, and nobody but a deadly gunfighter would have charged us sober."

"If it really was him," Ulysses said, "then I sure want to brace him."

"Don't be stupid," Mitch said. "I'd have expected Jud to say something like that, but not someone as smart as you are."

"I don't believe anyone can outdraw me." Ulysses said. "And I ain't afraid of the Gunsmith."

Mitch curbed his tongue, for it was not wise to insult Ulysses. Still, he knew that Ulysses was making a fool's talk. Only a young fool looking for a quick reputation would be stupid enough to brace a legend in a stand-up gunfight.

A turkey buzzard sailed high overhead, and Mitch pulled off his Stetson and sleeved his damp forehead. He was hot, and the wound in his side hurt like the dickens. Still, if he were correct, and it had been the Gunsmith who had charged them just south of Candelaria, they had been lucky that only Jud had gotten himself killed. And Jud, even though he was the baby of the family, had always been an accident just waiting to happen. Mitch was surprised that his youngest brother, with his arrogance and quick temper, hadn't gotten himself killed a long time ago.

"Let's ride," Ulysses said. "Ain't but a couple of miles yet to go."

Mitch put the spurs to his sweaty horse. It was almost sundown but it was still so damned hot that the heat waves were undulating. He would be glad to reach their hidden oasis, where a cold-water spring ran out of their huge rock dugout. Back inside the dugout, the air was damp from the spring, and it was cool and dim. Cool enough for a man to think he was resting up in the Sierras, where it was easy to sleep and dream of good whiskey and bad, bad women. Or even a good whiskey and good women, ones like Molly Malloy.

Just thinking of Molly make his pecker perk up real quick. Mitch actually smiled. It had been along time since he'd had a piece of pretty Molly. She was a widow now and well broken in to a man, but that was just fine. And one of these days. . . .

"There it is," Hank said, pointing up ahead toward a huge mound of rocks at the end of the broad, sage-covered valley. "Indian better be there watching things."

Indian was Paiute, a man who might be twenty or forty, it was impossible to tell. He was short, but very quick and a dead shot. He was also one of the best trackers and hunters Mitch had ever seen. Indian had staggered into Death Valley about two years ago, more dead than alive. There had been terrible rope burns around his neck, which had healed badly, leaving scars. Mitch figured Indian had been up to something and had been caught, lynched, and left for dead. But after his would-be executioners had cut him down and ridden away, leaving him for dead, Indian had still been alive. Blinded by pain and fear, Indian had headed into the desert, and blind luck had saved his life when he'd come across the Pike brothers.

They all considered Indian a good-luck charm. Hell, Jud had even rubbed Indian's dirty arm before they'd gone on a raid somewhere in California, Arizona, or Nevada. But obviously Indian was not lucky, because Jud, the one who had put the most store in Indian's good luck, had got himself killed.

Ulysses chuckled as they trotted the last blistering miles to the oasis. "Hell, you'll never know if Indian is there or not until *he* decides. "I'll bet that dirty bastard has us right square in the sights of his old rifle."

Mitch nodded because he was sure that was true. They fed Indian and allowed him to stay at the oasis not only because he was good medicine, but because the man would kill anyone who came near the place in their absence. And when they were hiding from the law, they could not have found a better guard than Indian, who seemed never to sleep. He ate little, did not drink more than his share and, from all indication, seemed content to spend the rest of his life watching over the oasis, their supplies, and the grain for the horses, as well as this blistering valley, which he considered his own private reservation.

"There he is," Hank said. Hank had the best eye of all of the brothers, and so Mitch just nodded. A few minutes later, Indian emerged from the rocks and waved at them. He was grinning.

"Bastard probably expects we've got whiskey," Ulysses growled. He's going to be damned disappointed to learn that all we got is money. No supplies or women or nothing."

"He'll live," Mitch said, punishing his horse by spurring it into a gallop.

His brothers came up hard behind him, and when they reached the rocks, at a place where it appeared there was no opening, suddenly they were charging through a narrow cleft and up a steep path to the small, hidden place no more than an acre in size, where their secret desert spring fed grass.

After they had passed inside, Indian laid some poles across the entrance to keep the horses from wandering outside. To wander into Death Valley was to die; Indian did not have much regard for the intelligence of horses, and so he made sure they stayed close.

The Pike brothers had taught him a few words of English, and he'd come knowing a few more, but their conversation was mostly sign language and plenty of grunts.

"No whiskey," Hank said, grinning, because he was always trying to change Indian's fixed and very blank expression. "No damn whiskey for Indian."

Indian shrugged his shoulders to say that he did not care.

"No women, either," Hank said, rocking his hips back and forth lewdly.

Again, Indian just shrugged. This annoyed Hank, who did not like the way Indian smelled. "No food, either," he said grimly.

Indian made sign language to show that he would go out into the desert with his bow and arrows and kill some jack rabbits. Indian did have a rifle, but it was an old single-shot percussion piece, and he did not like to waste powder or ball on rabbits. He saved his rifle for the hunting of men.

"Unsaddle the horses first," Mitch ordered, untying his saddlebags stuffed with stolen money. "Then go kill us some sage hens or rattlesnakes for supper. None of those damn wormy jack rabbits."

Indian understood enough to know what was being said. He nodded and went to work, while Mitch, Hank, and Ulysses ducked inside the rock dugout and moved deep inside, where the air seemed actually cold by comparison to what they had been enduring all day.

"Hey!" Mitch shouted, stopping in mid-stride so suddenly that Hank walked into the back of him. "Someone is in here!"

A gun materialized in Ulysses' hand as if by magic, but he lowered it a second later and said, "It's just a girl."

"Well, I'll be damned," Mitch said. "And she's white."

Hank licked his lips, then reached for his gunbelt, which he began to unbuckle. "She looks old enough for a man."

"No!" Mitch said. "She ain't but about twelve years old."

"He's right," Ulysses said. "Leave her be, Hank. Even Molly was older than that when we first started diddling her. This one's still too damned young."

Mitch moved forward. The girl was pressed up against the back wall, and her eyes were round with terror. Mitch tried to talk nice. "What's your name?"

The little girl's mouth worked silently.

"What the hell is the matter with her?" Hank growled. "She simple or something?"

"She's scared, is what she is," Mitch said. He made himself smile, and when he got to within a few feet of her, he repeated, "What's your name?"

"Annie," the girl whispered. "Annie Wakefield."

"How old are you?"

"Twelve."

"See?" Mitch said triumphantly. "I told you she was too young. She's only twelve."

"Bet she could still do it," Hank groused.

"You keep your hands off her!" Mitch warned, not raising his voice, because he did not want to frighten the little girl any more than she already was.

"Ask her why she's here," Ulysses urged.

"Annie, what are you doing here?"

Her eyes filled with tears. "That Indian, he killed my pa! Shot him with an arrow through the neck and then finished him off with his knife!"

Mitch frowned. "What was your pa doing in the valley?"

"Prospecting," the girl said. "And he found some gold, too."

"He did? Where?"

The girl studied them closely, and finally she said, "I don't exactly remember."

"Could you find it again?"

The girl squirmed under their gaze. Mitch could almost see her mind working hard in an effort to come up with the right answer. He took a quick step forward and grabbed her by the arm and shook her hard.

"Dammit! Don't you even think about lying to me, girl!"

Tears welled up in Annie's eyes, and she nodded. "I can find it."

Mitch pushed her away and grinned broadly. "Boys," he said to his brothers, "not only do we have over twelve thousand dollars in cash, but maybe—just maybe—we even have ourselves a gold mine!"

"But no damn whiskey," Hank said with dejection.

"Don't count on that," Mitch said, suddenly feeling very expansive. "I've got a little cache hidden out in the sagebrush."

"What!" Ulysses stormed.

"You heard me. Hell, if I left it here, how much do you think the Indian would leave for us?"

Hank and Ulysses exchanged glances, and then they grinned. It seemed to them, just as it seemed to Mitch, that everything was going their way.

SEVEN

They had ridden all night, and, if there had not been a full moon, the Gunsmith would not have been able to follow the tracks of the Pike brothers as they rode southwest across the Nevada border into the wasteland that was called Death Valley. Even at night the air was stiflingly hot, and Clint kept a close watch on Duke to make sure the gelding did not overextend himself. But the animal seemed to have no lingering problems as the result of the neck crease, and Clint stopped every three hours for water.

They had brought sixty gallons of water in goatskin bags. Each man carried twenty gallons strung across his saddlehorn, but given the heat and the amount it took to keep a horse from dehydrating, twenty gallons each was nothing at all. If they rationed the water carefully, they'd still run out in less then three days.

When dawn finally broke across Death Valley, the sun lifted out of the eastern horizon like a burning ember, and the temperature soared. This was a hellish place, even at sunrise, with the land rose colored. Clint had once chased an outlaw named Harry Carnes into Death Valley, and he had never forgotten the harsh, unforgiving nature of this country. The valley's western wall was formed by the Panamint Range, a line of corroded mountains that lifted nearly six thousand feet. The Grapevine, the Funeral, and the Black Mountains formed the eastern wall of the valley, and when heavy rains fell on their slopes, sudden flash floods could be more dangerous than the land itself. The Indians called this place *Tomesha*, which meant "ground afire," and Clint figured that was a very apt description, because in the summertime the rocks stored the day's awful heat so that the summer temperatures never cooled.

There was no graze for horses. The valley floor was either covered with creosote brush and sage, or else it was streaked with alkali or salt bed, which broke under a horse's hooves like old, crusted bread. When the wind blew, as it often did in the afternoons, it caused both these abrasive minerals to fill a man's eyes and the creases of his skin until he suffered with every movement and his eyes wept constantly.

Clint reined in his horse, dismounted, and said, "Let's give 'em another few gulps."

He poured a gallon of water into his hat and let Duke drink thirstily, then he took a couple of gulps for himself and capped the goatskin bag. "I wish I knew how far into this desert the Pike brothers were going."

"Can't be all that far," Jacobs said. "When they raced out of Candelaria, they sure weren't toting much water. I'd say that they have to be right at the northern edge of Death Valley."

Clint agreed with the blacksmith. The way he had it figured, the horses the Pike brothers had ridden into Candelaria had already been overheated. The fools had not watered them in town, so that meant that they could not go more than another full day without water.

"We'll come upon them by noon," Clint predicted. "Early afternoon at the latest."

Eubanks, the Wells Fargo manager, was flushed from the heat. He was not a man accustomed to long hours in the saddle, and the all-night ride had taken its toll. "I sure don't want to go much farther into this hell," he crabbed. "A man could die plenty easy if his horse lamed up."

"If he throws a shoe, I can fix it," the blacksmith said. "It does no good to think about everything that could go wrong. And there's something else: I think you're drinking way too much water."

Eubanks bristled. "You just mind your business and I'll mind mine, and we'll let it go at that."

Clint lined out in front, his eyes never straying from the tracks that he followed. He kept glancing up toward the mountains to the west, wondering exactly where the Pike brothers would take refuge. He had been a law man long enough to realize that the Pike brothers would build their dugout near water, but also someplace where they could at least hide their horses. For another thing, it seemed likely that their hiding place would either have to be down low in some valley, or else among the frequent piles of rock that were lined up like forgotten sentinels across the 140-mile-long valley floor.

Jacobs trotted up beside him. "You said we'd find them by noon. Hell, man, we can see in any direction for fifty miles or more."

Clint didn't even look at the man. "We can't see them yet, but they're close. They could be hiding anywhere. There might be a valley just beyond the next ridge, or a hideout in those rocks off to our right or left. So instead of talking, you'd be better off just to keep quiet and watch."

"Do you think they expect to be followed?"

"No," Clint said. "But out here, there's damn little chance of sneaking up on anyone. And we're easy targets for a man with a rifle and scope."

Without another word, Eubanks fell back behind Clint and Jacobs. He was still riding last in line when Indian, out hunting sage hens with his bow and arrow, saw the three men enter his valley.

Indian had not brought his rifle, and he did not for a moment consider trying to reach the oasis where the Pike brothers were now hiding. Instead, he dropped down into the brush and began to wriggle forward on a line that would bring him up behind the riders.

He crawled very fast and, had it not been for the fact that he chanced upon a rattlesnake, he would have timed his attack perfectly. But the rattler was as big around as his wrist, and it was in no mood to give ground to Indian. In fact, it was curled in the striking position, and its rattles sounded an ominous warning.

Indian considered retreating and then circling around the viper, but when he lifted his head just above the brush, he saw that he had no time to circle the snake. Indian ducked back down in the brush, drew his knife, and waved his left hand in the rattler's face. Just as he expected, the big snake struck, its thick body flying out with fangs exposed. Indian jerked his hand away, and when the snake missed and was fully extended, the blade in Indian's right hand flashed, and the rattler's head was severed cleanly from its slick, muscular body, which wriggled and flopped in violent convulsions. The rattlers head also died hard. Its jaws and the long, poisonous fangs continued to bite for several minutes after Indian slid by the viper and continued forward.

When Indian reached the back trail of the three riders, he lifted his bow from the place where it had been slung over his shoulder alongside his quiver. He selected, then nocked an arrow, and slowly came to his feet. The nearest

rider moving away was Ernie Eubanks; Indian drew the
arrow back until his bow bent nearly to breaking, and then
he released his bowstring. Even before his arrow thudded
into the rider's back and caused him to cry out and lift up
in his stirrups, Indian was reaching for another arrow. He
would next kill the big one, who was still riding ahead
without any clue as to his own danger.

Clint heard Eubank's grunt of pain, and when he turned,
he saw two things happening. The Wells Fargo manager
was toppling out of his saddle, and an Indian was nocking
a second arrow for another kill.

Clint knew that a gunshot might bring the Pike brothers
out of their hiding, and that would be the end of everything. So instead of drawing his gun, he drove Duke forward, but was too late to keep the Indian from unleashing a
second arrow. He passed Jacobs just as the blacksmith
groaned and took an arrow in his back. The Gunsmith
cursed with fury and sent his horse crashing into the Indian, knocking him down into the brush. Clint brought his
horse to a sliding stop and then bailed out of his saddle.
The Indian was dazed, but had the sense to realize that he
could not hope to use his bow and arrow a third time. The
Indian drew his knife and Clint drew his gun. They both
lashed out; the Gunsmith's arm was two inches longer, and
that was the difference. The barrel of his Colt caught the
Indian across his nose and broke it with a sickening
crunch. They barreled into each other's arms and rolled
into the brush. The Indian tried to bury his blade in the
Gunsmith, but Clint caught the man's wrist and twisted the
knife around. For an instant, their bodies shook with exertion, and then the Gunsmith's superior strength prevailed,
and he drove the knife into the Indian's chest. The Indian
shuddered and was still.

Clint hurled the Indian's knife into the brush and

climbed unsteadily to his feet to see Jacobs slumped over in his saddle, his face white with pain. "Did you get him?"

"Yeah," Clint said. "Get down off that horse and let me have a look at that arrow sticking out of your back."

"It feels like a lance!" the blacksmith said, as he nearly toppled off his horse.

Clint used his knife to cut the blacksmith's shirt away from the wound. It was bleeding heavily, but Clint was sure that it had been stopped from penetrating a lung by the blacksmith's shoulder blade. "If I pull it out, you will probably bleed to death."

"Then just break the shaft off and leave it be." Jacobs said.

Clint took the shaft in both hands and broke it about an inch from the man's flesh. "We've got to get you to a doctor," Clint said. "And we've got to do it fast."

"But what about the Pike brothers?"

"They're going to have to wait. With any luck, they still don't know we're after them. I can come back later."

"But—"

"But nothing," Clint swore. "Let's get out of here before we find ourselves outgunned and in a worse mess than we are already."

Jacobs, his face ashen, nodded. He felt sick and already weak. It was all he could do to climb back into his saddle and watch as Clint hoisted Ernie Eubanks across his own saddle.

Clint mounted. Eubank's horse would trail after them all the way back to Candelaria. Clint hoped that the blacksmith could hang on until they reached a doctor. Otherwise he might have two dead men by the time he reached Candelaria. Two men who'd died trying to impress the women they loved.

That would be one hell of a grim note.

EIGHT

Clint wearily approached Candelaria late the next afternoon, grim-faced and dreading the reception he'd face. When he entered the main street, he rode straight up to the doctor's office and helped big Heck Jacobs down from his horse. The blacksmith's face was pinched with suffering, and he looked as if he had aged ten years because of the arrow protruding from his back.

A crowd gathered very quickly, and it stared at the body of Ernie Eubanks just as it had the first time Clint had entered Candelaria and watched a morbid crowd stare at four dead townsmen gunned down after the Pike brothers had robbed their bank.

"Somebody quit gawkin' and get him over to the mortician's office!" Clint snapped. "Dammit, but I never seen folks like you."

The mayor, Roy Perkins, was highly agitated. "I told you to just let things be. Now we've lost Mr. Eubanks, and the blacksmith don't look like he's going to pull through, either."

"Shut up," the blacksmith choked, clinging to his saddlehorn as he found his legs and decided he was still strong enough to walk. "If it hadn't been for the Gunsmith, I'd be dead right now."

Clint put a shoulder under the blacksmith's arm and helped him into the doctor's office, but not before he heard a cry and glanced over his shoulder to see Ruth Eubanks throw herself at her husband's body and begin to sob. It took several men to pull her away, and some women led her off down the street.

The doctor was middle-aged, pudgy, had sorrowful eyes, and whiskey on his breath, but he wasted no time in getting big Heck Jacobs onto his examining table.

Clint leaned forward. "What do you think, Doc? Is he. . . ."

"Hard to say. You did the right thing to leave the arrow be. From his color, I'd say he's already lost a lot of blood."

Jacobs turned his head sideways and growled, "I didn't ride out of Death Valley to die in your office, Doc. So quit the jawin' and get that damned thing out of me."

"You just hang on a couple of minutes, and then you'll wish you had already died," the doctor said with mock gruffness. "It's going to hurt like blazes. Be better if you had a bottle of whiskey to pull on."

"The hell with the whiskey! Do it!"

"You always were a loud and impatient man," the doctor said, getting a large set of forceps and a scalpel. "Now, don't you take a swing at me when I yank on this thing."

Jacobs gritted his teeth, and Clint watched as the doctor reached into a drawer and extracted a fifth of whiskey. Instead of offering it to his patient, however, he took a long pull on it himself, smacked his lips, and said in a gravely voice, "Steadies the hand, you know. Help yourself, Gunsmith."

Clint had the need of a drink. The whiskey burned away the salt and alkali in his throat. He was aware that he must have looked mighty rough and ill-used. His eyes were leaking and swollen, his lips were cracked by the heat and the sun, and the folds of skin where his joints met were raw and inflamed. Somehow, the alkali had even gotten into his crotch, and it was painful to walk.

"Have another pull, especially if you intend to watch this," the doctor said.

Clint gladly took another pull, the doctor followed suit, and then Jacobs himself finished the whiskey and said, "If we're gonna get drunk, let's do it in a saloon, not in a damned doctor's office!"

The doctor brought a basin of water over and said, "Hang on to the table and don't move. You're too big to strap down, so I've got to trust you."

Jacobs gripped the table, and he humped up like a camel when the doctor's scalpel sliced deep into his flesh, making a pair of incisions outward from wound in opposite directions. "Grab ahold of the wooden shaft," the doctor said to Clint.

Clint grabbed ahold of the broken-off shaft, and the doctor stuck his big forceps down into the flowing wound and closed his eyes. It was obvious that he was feeling for the arrowhead and wanted to make damn sure it came out with the shaft.

"I think I've got it," he whispered as Jacobs squirmed in mute agony. "Now, slow and easy, let's pull it out."

The arrowhead was firmly embedded in muscle, and it was surprisingly difficult to pull free. The doctor had to use his scalpel once more, and then the arrowhead tore loose and came out clean.

"Ugghh!" Jacobs moaned through clenched teeth.

Clint hurled the arrow behind him before he realized that it struck Molly's dress. She didn't seem to notice, however, as she came forward and used a silk handkerchief to mop the blacksmith's brow. "Heck Jacobs, you're coming over to my hotel and recuperate," she said in a way that left no room for argument. "You're going to take a bath, and I'm going to make sure you have a clean room, clean sheets, and some clean clothes for a change."

Heck smiled weakly. He was in no shape to argue.

Both Clint and the woman stood back and watched as the doctor worked slowly but skillfully to cleanse the arrow wound and then bandage it tightly. When the doctor was finished, he took out a second bottle and said, "This is going to cost you a month's board of my horse, Jacobs. A whole month."

"I'll stand the loss," the blacksmith said. "Especially if you'll give me a little taste of that second bottle."

Clint and Molly left the doctor's office and pushed through the waiting crowd, which had stationed itself outside the doctor's office.

"He's going to be all right," Clint said.

"Yeah, well, what about the Pike brothers?" a fat man wearing a brown suit and derby challenged.

The Gunsmith walked over to the thirsty, exhausted horses that had carried them into and out of Death Valley. He took Duke's reins and those of the other two animals and led them over to a water trough. The animals had lost a good hundred pounds each, but the Gunsmith knew that their weight would come back quickly.

"Well, Gunsmith!" the fat man barked, "What about them?"

Clint stared hard at the man. "I'm going back down into Death Valley," he said. "Only this next time, I'm going to bring the Pikes back—dead, or alive. And you know what else?"

"What?"

Clint forced a cold grin. "I'm going to call for a posse this time. And I want *you* to be the first to volunteer."

The fat man blanched, spun on his heels, and fled into the crowd.

"It seems he didn't have as much guts as he had mouth," Clint observed loudly. "Who's going to be the first man to step forward and make a posse?"

The miners and storekeepers, freighters and drifters, all shrank back under the Gunsmith's hard stare.

Clint shook his head. "You are the sorriest bunch of folks I ever come across. I'll tell you one thing, though. If I manage to bring the Pike brothers back alive to stand trial, there had better be nine good men willing to make up a hanging jury. Because if there isn't, ther's going to be hell to pay before I shake off the dust of Candelaria for the last time."

Molly took his arm and pulled him away from the crowd. "Come on," she said. "Let's take care of these horses, and then let's take care of you."

Clint didn't resist. In an effort to ease the pain between his legs, he walked sort of bow-legged. He figured that he needed a lot of taking care of. But one thing for sure, watching the doctor pull that arrow out of big Heck Jacobs had made him all the more determined to find the Pike brothers and settle the score.

They found box stalls for the three horses, and the old man whom Heck Jacobs had hired to oversee his stable seemed only too glad to promise that he'd rub all three animals down, then curry and grain them heavily.

"I'll get them back to the way they was a couple of days ago, when you boys rode south," he vowed. "You bet I will."

"Take special care of my black," Clint said, pitching the man a silver dollar. "That horse is going to have to carry me back to Death Valley as soon as I'm up to riding."

"You going back? What the hell for?"

Clint sleeved the tears from his burning eyes and said, "Because I got a job to finish, Old Timer. And a man should always finish what he starts. Ain't that so?"

The old geezer broke into a wide grin, revealing that he was missing more teeth than he still owned. "Damn right it is!"

Clint took Molly's arm and headed for her hotel. The first thing he wanted was a hot bath, and the second was a big steak with some more whiskey. No, come to think of it, the second thing he wanted was the pretty woman between some soft, clean bedsheets.

NINE

Clint was still soaking in the bathtub when a loud knocking sounded on Molly's door.

Molly, who had been scrubbing Clint's back, stood up and walked to the door. "Who is it?"

"Ruth Eubanks. I have to talk to the Gunsmith."

"He's busy right now," Molly said, her voice leaving no doubt that she did not care for the woman.

"I'll just bet he is. Let me talk to him anyway."

"He's in the damn bath, Ruth!"

"Open the door!"

"The hell with it," Molly snapped. "If she wants to see you that badly, who am I to stop her?"

Before Clint could protest, Molly had unlocked the door and let the woman inside. Ruth was already dressed in a black dress to signify that she was deep in mourning. But for a young woman who'd just lost her husband, she looked uncommonly attractive. Sweeping past Molly, she marched right up to the Gunsmith, who sank down in the tub.

"You're going to have to write up a report for my husband's company, explaining how he lost his life trying to retrieve Wells Fargo money."

There was not enough water in the tub, and Clint found himself pressing the bottom hard. Even so, he had to cross his hands over his privates to attain some small measure of modesty.

Clint found it hard to reason with the widow in black who looked down at him in the bathtub. "Well, sure!" he stammered. "I'll be happy to do that."

Mrs. Eubanks did not seem even to hear him. She acted as if she expected a fight. "And another thing: I thought that a man of your reputation would be able to protect my husband! But you didn't. You got him killed, and you didn't even arrest or shoot those damn Pike brothers."

Clint colored with anger. He forgot about his penis, which kept floating to the surface like a stick of redwood, and he sputtered, "Well dammit, I never wanted your husband along in the first place! And if you hadn't pushed him into coming so he could get a commendation and company promotion, he'd be alive today."

Ruth stiffened as if she had been kicked in the belly. "That's not true!" she cried.

"Oh, yes it is! I walked into his office and heard you giving him hell for not doing more to gain a damned promotion. So as far as his death is concerned, Mrs. Eubanks, I hold you every bit as responsible as I hold myself."

Tears welled up in Ruth's large brown eyes. "I hate you!" she cried, bending at the waist and swinging her fist at him.

Clint caught her by the wrist and pulled her into the tub. It wasn't something he'd intended to do; it was just a reaction and it happened. The woman clawed at his face, and it was all Clint could do to push her away and then stand up and grab her by the arms.

Ruth looked down at his red and swollen manhood and screeched like a cat. She doubled up her fist and took another big swing at him, but Clint ducked, slipped, and crashed back into the tub, pulling the fighting woman back in with him.

"Molly," he shouted, "don't just stand there gaping at us. Help me get rid this woman!"

Molly finally jumped into the action. She grabbed the soaking-wet Ruth Eubanks from behind and wrestled her kicking and screaming out the door.

Clint splashed water into his face. "Damn," he whispered, "I'd rather take on all three of the Pikes at once than be naked in a bathtub and face that woman again."

Molly just stared at him and then she began to laugh.

Clint did not see the Eubanks widow until the day he was ready to return to Death Valley. He was saddling Duke and making a final check on his gear when he heard the barn door creak behind him and turned to see Ruth standing in a big pane of sunlight that cut diagonally through the barn door. A sunlight that revealed the bright amber highlights in her hair.

He wondered if she had come to shoot him or attack him with her fists, but when she raised her hands and then dropped them helplessly to her side, he decided that she had come to do neither.

"I hear you are leaving and no one in Candelaria will go with you," she said quietly.

Clint leaned across his saddle. "I took two brave men the last time, and look what happened to them. Sometimes a man is better off working alone. It's what I know best, anyway."

"It isn't fair," Ruth said, taking a few tentative steps

until she was standing in the dimness. It wasn't your money or your kinfolk that the Pike brothers robbed and murdered here. It was ours, and we should be riding out in force instead of hanging back and making excuses."

Clint wound his fingers through Duke's mane. "There isn't a whole lot in life that is fair, Ruth. It wasn't fair that your husband died."

She swallowed noisily, and her eyes drifted away for a moment. "The house seems so quiet now, I wake up alone in the dark and realize how much I miss him. I didn't think I would miss him so much. He was a good man."

"Yeah, I know."

Ruth came and touched Duke's shoulder. "What happened? Did he die . . . easy?"

"Yes, he did. Arrow caught him in the back. He died instantly."

She closed her eyes, and he saw a tear slide down her cheek. "I blame no one but myself. That's what I came to say."

Clint reached impulsively across his saddle and touched her cheek. "Blaming won't help. It'll just make the pain and the loss worse. You've got to bury all that and go on with your life."

She shook her head. "I'm going to sell our house. As soon as it sells, I'm going back to Indiana to live with my family. I never should have married Ernie and come out to this Nevada Territory. I've hated it since the day we arrived. I guess that hatred was why I pushed my late husband so hard for a promotion."

Clint nodded and busied himself tightening his cinch.

"I hear that Mrs. Malloy is taking good care of Heck Jacobs. Watching over him day . . . and night."

Clint looked up to meet the woman's eyes. "Is that what you hear?"

"Yes."

"She runs her hotel and watches over him during the day—but not during the night."

Ruth could not hide her disappointment. "Oh. I see."

Clint slipped under Duke's neck and cupped the woman's face in his hands. "What did you *really* come to say to me?"

Her eyes grew round and misty. "I came to tell you not to go after those terrible men all alone. I came to say that I don't want you killed like my husband. It wasn't your money, and you shouldn't die for it."

"I don't intend to die," Clint said, pulling the woman close against his chest.

"I. . . I want you to stay here, and when I sell my house, I thought maybe we could go away someplace together."

A smile crept across the Gunsmith's face. "Why, Ruth! The last time you came to tell me something, you ended up by trying to scratch my eyes out or drown me. What happened?"

"I went crazy," she whispered. "I was sick with guilt, and I lost my head. I knew it even when I tried to hurt you, but that didn't keep me from going crazy."

The Gunsmith covered her mouth with his own. He felt her tongue pushing at his lips, and he opened his mouth and drew it inside and felt her body swaying against hers. What he really wanted to do was not to go after the Pike brothers, but to carry Ruth over to a pile of fresh straw and make love to her.

"I better ride out now," he said, forcing himself to pull away.

"Why?" Her hands were pulling at his shirt. "Oh, Clint! Stay. Please!"

"No," he said, mounting his horse while he still had a shred of will power. "If I made love to you without trying to kill or capture the Pikes, well, I'd feel guilty as sin."

"But they didn't kill my husband. He was shot by an Indian!"

"*Their* Indian," Clint said. "I've thought about it, and I know that was the case. We had to be close to where they were hiding. Real close."

Clint reached down and fingered the woman's hair. "Molly Malloy is going to fall in love with the right man this time, and the right man is Heck Jacobs. I know that, even if she doesn't."

"Then if you come back, it will be to me?"

"*When* I come back," Clint said as he galloped off to a showdown in Death Valley.

TEN

The very last thing in the world Clint wanted to do was to return to the punishing heat of Death Valley. Still, he was a man who firmly believed in his own abilities, and also that once a thing was started, it ought to be seen through to the finish, no matter how difficult or dangerous.

Being alone, he traveled faster this time, riding at a steady trot, which carried him to the place where the Indian had suddenly risen out of the brush and managed to unleash two arrows.

The Indian's body was gone, just as Clint had suspected it would be. There was not even a trace of blood or a sign of the struggle where they had fought to the death. Clint squatted on his heels and examined the ground very carefully. If a man knew what he was looking for, it was not hard to see how a branch of sagebrush had been used to wipe out every physical sign of men in a death struggle.

Clint remained motionless for nearly ten minutes as his

eyes surveyed the land and the direction that seemed most likely the Pike brothers had taken when they'd carried off the Indian's body. He knew that he had lost his only advantage—the element of surprise. Now the Pike brothers would be expecting him, or someone else, and they would be wary. They would have read the tracks that he, Eubanks, and the blacksmith had left, and determined that their horses had been shod. That would have told them that it had been white men who had killed their Indian. No doubt they'd also have followed the tracks north until they were certain that the white men had come from the direction of Candelaria. If they put two and two together, they might even come to suspect that it was the man on the black horse, who'd challenged them before and would challenge them again.

"I wonder if they know who I am?" the Gunsmith said to himself as he stood up and tried to guess which one of the many deep *arroyos* or great masses of piled boulders, could hide an oasis fed by a deep underground spring.

Clint decided to follow the brushed-out tracks until this vital question was revealed to him, and then to sit out the rest of the day. After dark, he could move in and take his chances.

Instead of remounting, he led Duke through the sage, and several times when the ground turned especially rocky, he had to drop down on his knees to follow the tracks of the Pike brothers. With agonizing slowness, he covered a mile, then two miles, and just as darkness was falling, he looked ahead and decided he was quite certain where the Pike brothers were hiding. There was a jutting mountain of rocks bigger than the others he'd ridden past. Clint estimated that the rocks might be piled several hundred feet high and were at least a mile in circumference.

This had to be the place the Pike brothers had described to Molly Malloy. Clint could see no other geological for-

mation for at least twenty miles which would offer any
possiblity of a hidden oasis in this terrible desert.

Were they already watching him across the perhaps
three-mile stretch of wasteland that separated him from the
cathedral of granite and sandstone rock? Clint had no way
of knowing the answer to that question. He figured he
would have to assume they were, and that they'd be ready
and waiting.

Three-to-one odds were long, but he'd faced worse.
And maybe he'd inflicted a couple of disabling bullet
wounds on the Pike brothers. But he doubted it.

Pulling his hat down low on his forehead, Clint loos-
ened his cinch and then gave himself and Duke a drink of
water. He stared at the great pile of rocks up ahead, then
patted his horse and said, "If I'm right and lucky, before
dawn we'll be drinking cool water and you'll be eating
green grass."

Hesitating, he frowned and said, "But if I'm wrong or
unlucky, for me there won't be even a tomorrow."

Three miles south, Mitch stood up from the campfire
and tossed his dirty plate of beans and tortillas to the
ground. "Without Indian, we're going to be damned hard-
pressed to come up with any kind of fresh meat out here."

Ulysses looked up from his plate. "If it was the
Gunsmith who killed Indian, then we'd better be expecting
visitors. You know that a good tracker won't be stopped or
fooled by us brushing out our tracks. Thing of it is, me and
Hank feel like we ought to either ride for Candelaria and
settle this business, or split up our money and head for
California."

The giant nodded. "I don't understand why we're still
waitin' around here."

"Because," Mitch snapped, "the girl said her father had discovered gold in Death Valley."

"Which we ain't found a trace of it yet," Ulysses said, glaring at the girl, who crouched at the edge of their campfire. "I think she's lying."

"Now why would she do that?" Mitch asked softly, his eyes watching those of the girl for any change in expression that would betray her true thoughts.

"'Cause she's afraid we'll kill her if she's worth nothing."

Secretly, Mitch was beginning to think the same thing, though he did not want to admit that to his brothers. "We'll give her one more day to find the place."

He stepped over to the girl and stabbed a finger downward at her. "You hear me, Annie?" he shouted. "We find gold tomorrow or you're going to be coyote meat. You understand that?"

The girl nodded. She had never been so afraid in her entire life, and it seemed to her that she had to escape in the darkness, because there was no gold. Never had been. Ulysses had guessed right when he said she was lying to save her own hide. But the lying wouldn't work past tomorrow, and Annie believed they really would kill her if she did not run tonight.

"Hank, hike up in the rocks and take a look before the sun goes down," Mitch ordered.

"Dammit! Why is it always me?" the giant bawled.

"Because you got the best eyes in the family," Mitch said. "You can see things that me and Ulysses can't see at all."

The answer pleased Hank just as much as it always did. Other than his brute strength, his eyesight was his only superior quality. "All right," he said in a grudging tone of voice. "But tomorrow, someone else is taking a turn. You and Ulysses can go keep lookout."

"No," Mitch said, "tomorrow Annie is going to finally show us her father's gold mine. Isn't that right?"

Annie nodded. It was almost dark. She could hardly wait to run.

ELEVEN

Clint gazed up at the stars and judged it to be around eleven o'clock. The moon cast its soft, golden glow across the desert, and the great fortress of rock lifted in a dark silhouette above the baking desert floor. The Gunsmith checked his weapon and tightened his cinch. He jammed his foot in his stirrup and swung up into the saddle.

It was time for a showdown.

Clint had no intention of riding directly toward the rocks. Instead, he reined Duke to the west and made a five-mile loop which brought him up near the south end of the rocks, where he dismounted and then slowly moved forward to tie his horse where it could not be seen.

He watered Duke from the goatskin bag and took a few gulps himself before stepping onto the rocks, which he immediately began to climb. The going was slow, and the rocks were hot to the touch, but the Gunsmith felt sure that he had found the Pike brothers' Death Valley hideout. That feeling grew stronger when he climbed over the crown of rocks and then knelt to witness the grassy oasis nestled below.

A horse lifted its head suddenly and whinnied at the Gunsmith. Clint pressed in next to a stunted juniper pine and waited until the animals resumed grazing. He shook his head in wonder, because finding such a place as this in Death Valley seemed like a miracle. All during the previous late afternoon, he had stared at this, as well as other rock formations, and he hadn't seen any indication that there was even an entrance into this cone-shaped valley, much less that the desert would give precious water.

Clint took his time descending from the rimmed wall of high rocks. He had not yet located the dugout described by Molly, but he knew it could not be far away. When he reached the little meadow, he dropped into a crouch and moved forward slowly, his eyes constantly rotating back and forth.

Five minutes later he spotted the opening of the dugout, and now he found a hiding place as he considered his next move. He did not particularly relish the idea of going inside the dugout, because it would be dark and unfamiliar. Once inside, he'd not only be at a numerical disadvantage, but blind as well.

The Gunsmith considered his options very carefully. In the end he decided that he would wait all night, then get the drop on the Pike brothers at dawn by positioning himself just outside their door. When they came outside, he'd catch them totally by surprise. If that Indian had still been alive, the plan would have had no chance at all, but with him out of the picture, it seemed entirely possible to catch all three brothers off guard.

Clint was about to move into position, when suddenly he saw a figure appear in the open doorway of the dugout. The Gunsmith flattened against the rocks and then gaped, because it was immediately apparent that he was looking at a small girl.

What the hell was a little girl doing inside a place like that?

Clint holstered his gun and watched from hiding as the girl tiptoed out from the dugout, and when she was about twenty feet from its door, she bolted and went scurrying across the moonlit meadow. She was so frightened that she spooked the grazing horses, which galloped away with their tails in the air. The thundering of their hooves broke the night silence, and Clint heard the little girl cry out in fear just before she vanished into the far rocks.

The Gunsmith was just about to go after her when the Pike brothers burst out of their dugout.

"Where the hell did she go?" one yelled.

"How the hell should I know!"

"Spread out. Hank, you search every inch of the meadow: Ulysses, you swing to the left, and I'll loop around to the right. We'll catch her before we meet on the far wall."

Ulysses did not appreciate the idea. "Why the hell don't we just let her go and find her come daybreak? She ain't going anywhere in this desert, Mitch. Not on foot, she isn't."

The one named Mitch paused a moment, then said, "No, we need to find her right away. She could steal a horse, and then where'd we be?"

Clint had already learned everything that he could about the Pike brothers, and now he had no difficulty identifying Mitch as the leader, Ulysses as the gunfighter, and the giant who'd been assigned to search the meadow as the one named Hank.

Clint knew that Ulysses was the man whom he had to watch most carefully. He'd be snake-quick with his gun. As the three men separated, Clint figured he could not have

asked for a better situation. He slipped out from behind his
cover and went after Ulysses, moving as silently as he
could. It was to his great advantage that the damned
spooky horses were still galloping noisily around and
around the grassy meadow.

The Gunsmith went after Ulysses in a hurry. He wanted,
and fully intended, to get this business over with just as
quickly as possible. If the Pike brothers managed to find
and grab the little girl, that would make things pretty dicey.
During the years he'd been a law man, Clint had been
faced with life-and-death situations, where a desperate
gunman had taken a hostage. It was always a sonofabitch
to figure out how to kill the gunman without unduly risking
the life of the hostage.

Ulysses was moving quickly himself, but the man was
so intent on recapturing the girl that every bit of his attention was focused on the ground and the rocks ahead of
him, making it a relatively simple task for the Gunsmith to
come up behind the man. Clint did not waste a moment in
hesitation. Gun in hand, he brought it slashing down
against the back of Ulysses' skull. He'd pistol-whipped a
lot of men in his time and knew when he felt the barrel of
his Colt strike solidly that Ulysses would be out cold for
hours. Even so, he disarmed the man before moving on to
complete the circle and come face-to-face with Mitch.

It took him nearly fifteen minutes to go halfway around
the rock wall, where he ducked behind some boulders and
waited for Mitch to come blundering into his trap.

He did not have long to wait. Mitch was out of breath
and breathing hard when he rushed past Clint, who stuck
out his foot and sent him sprawling headlong into the
rocks.

Mitch went for his gun. Clint's boot caught him in the
wrist and the man's gun sailed into the rocks to disappear.

"Ahhhh!" Mitch cried, looking up at the Gunsmith.

Clint jumped forward and drove the barrel of his six-gun into Mitch's throat. The man gagged, and then he froze and looked up at Clint to say, "You gotta be the Gunsmith."

"That's right," Clint said, cocking back the hammer of his gun. "Now call your overgrown brother and tell him you just found that little girl."

When Mitch hesitated, Clint jammed the barrel of his gun into this throat, and this time Mitch was a believer. "Hank!" he shouted. "Hank, I found Annie! Come on over here."

They both heard the giant come running. The man was so big, he sounded like a bull moose stomping across the plains. Clint turned to get the drop on Hank, saying, "One word of warning and you're both dead men. Understood?"

Mitch nodded. He was still having difficulty breathing after being jammed in the throat twice. Clint figured that alone would keep him occupied for the next few minutes.

The running footsteps slowed to a walk, and then stopped altogether. "Mitch, where are you?"

Clint pointed his Colt back at the outlaw leader. His meaning was very clear, and it caused Mitch to cry out in a hoarse voice, "I'm over here!"

"You got the girl?"

"Yeah," Mitch croaked. "I got her!"

Clint turned around and waited for Hank to appear, but when he did, the Gunsmith had the worst surprise of his life. The muzzle of Hank's Colt was pressed up against Annie's head.

Hank giggled sadistically. He held the wriggling girl against his chest with one massive forearm "*I* got her, not you. So drop your gun or I'll blow her brains all over these rocks."

Clint felt the bottom of his stomach drop to his feet. He heard Mitch choke with rage, and the Gunsmith knew that he was a dead man if he handed his gun over to this pair.

Maybe Annie, despite her terror, seemed to realize that she was also finished if she did not try something, because she bit Hank's arm. Sank her teeth into the flesh so deep that she thought she could feel his bones.

Hank screamed and dropped her, and that was the instant Clint fired and sent a bullet that passed through Hank's right shoulder.

The giant staggered back and began to bawl in agony, holding his shoulder as blood poured through his fingers. Mitch tried to tackle the Gunsmith, but he was on his belly, and a man cannot leap from that position.

"Freeze or die!" Clint hissed.

Mitch froze.

Clint looked over at the girl, who had fallen between some rocks. She was crying. He reached down with his free hand and pulled her to his side. "I'm going to help you," he said. "I'm going to help you find your family when we get out of here."

"I don't have any family! They're dead."

Clint did not know what to say for a minute, then he stroked the girl's hair and said, "You're very brave. And if you don't have a family, I'll find you a new one to love."

Annie threw her arms around his neck, and if Mitch hadn't still been prone on the ground, he might have gotten to the Gunsmith before Clint could free his Colt and get it aimed in Mitch's general direction.

Clint hugged the girl tightly. She stank and was very thin, and it made him so damned mad that, had he not been a man who believed in the law, he would have shot both the Pike brothers on the spot.

Instead he growled, "You rotten bastards are going to swing, all three of you."

"You got Ulysses?"

"Yeah," Clint said with grim satisfaction. "Your gunfighter is taking a long siesta. By the time he awakens, he'll be tied and roped together with you and the giant."

Mitch's lip curled with contempt. "You mean to take us back to Candelaria?"

"That's right."

"You'll never make it."

"Don't bet on it," Clint said. "A lot of tougher men than you have bet against me and they died for their foolishness."

The Gunsmith motioned the man to climb to his feet. "Go help your brother and let's see if he bleeds to death or not before we can get him to a doctor."

"You're a damned hard man," Mitch said, coming to his feet.

Clint hugged the little girl tightly. "And mister, you and your brothers are no better than animals. Now move!"

The Gunsmith kept his gun on Mitch, while somehow keeping his arm around the girl, who seemed never to want to let go of him. He finally got the two brothers down to their dugout and got the giant to quit hollering.

Clint hog-tied the pair so tightly that they could not move, and then he gave his gun to the girl, saying, "I have to get the other one, and then catch my own horse as well as the ones inside this place. "These men can't get free, but if they even try, you shoot them both. Understand?"

"Yes," Annie whispered.

"Good. I'll be back in a few minutes. We're not going to wait for daylight. We're going to get that stolen money and then get the he—the heck out of here."

For the first time, Annie managed to nod her head and smile, and that's when Clint knew that everything was going to work out just fine.

TWELVE

It was a day and a sight that the citizens of Candelaria agreed they would never forget when Clint and the little girl rode into town on Duke, prodding the three Pike brothers at the point of Clint's six-gun.

The brothers were roped neck to neck, a method Clint had seen used on runaway slaves before the Civil War, and one that was cruel, but effective. To the Gunsmith's way of reasoning, no southern black slave had ever deserved as harsh a treatment as the Pike brothers.

The townspeople, who had been so terrified of the Pikes, were stunned at the sight of the three pathetic creatures who swayed and shuffled up the main street of their town. They could scarcely believe the trio was really the notorious Pike brothers. But the more the citizens stared, the more convinced they were that their eyes were not betraying them.

Hank Pike, the sadistic giant who had often broken men

with his fists easily attracted the most attention. His shirt was drenched with blood from his shoulder wound, and he scared the living daylights out of the women and children.

Mitch and Ulysses were not disfigured, but they moved like zombies. Clint had herded the brothers all the way from Death Valley, and the hot desert sand had filtered into their boots to burn and blister their feet until they could barely walk. Roy Perkins, the mayor of Candelaria, was a man who was rarely without words, but the shocking appearance of the Pike brothers left him nearly speechless. Someone bumped Perkins forward, and he came to rest in front of the Pikes. He looked into their eyes and saw such pain and hatred that he jumped back and tripped over himself in his haste to get away.

Nobody laughed. Nobody even noticed, because all eyes were now on the Gunsmith. "Mayor," he said, "where's your bank president?"

"Right here!" a man called.

Clint tossed a pair of bulging saddlebags to the startled man. "I think you'll find it's all there to the cent. There sure isn't anyplace to spend it in Death Valley."

Nervous giggles filtered through the crowd as Clint continued, "Now where's Mrs. Eubanks?"

Ruth pushed through the crowd, making a point to avoid looking at the Pikes. When she'd caught a first glimpse of them and their suffering, joy had filled her heart, and she had wanted to laugh at their misery. Assailed by strong pangs of guilt shortly afterward, she had decided to avoid the sight of the three killers entirely.

"I'm here, Clint!"

The Gunsmith tossed her a package. "It's the money that was stolen from your husband's Wells Fargo office," he explained. "I thought that you'd want to be the one to return it to the company."

She looked deep into his eyes. "Thank you."

Clint turned his attention back to the mayor. "Perkins, since this town has no jail, I want you to hire a man to sink a big post in the center of this street, and get someone to forge a chain and shackles."

"I can do that free of charge," Heck Jacobs said, striding up the street with Molly in tow. "In fact, I insist on being the one to do it!"

More nervous chuckles. Clint looked into Molly's eyes, and he saw a difference in the way she returned his gaze. She'd already decided that Heck would be her next husband, that the Gunsmith was the kind that would never be tamed. Clint nodded to her and said, "I have a little surprise for you, Molly. Her name is Annie, and she has no family."

Molly looked at Annie, and without a word, she reached up and took the waif in her arms and beamed. "I can't think of anything that would make me happier," she said.

Clint felt mighty good about that. He even smiled before turning his attention back to the mayor and the gawking townspeople. "Since you folks are so good at watching instead of doing, I'm sure you'll take turns watching over the Pike brothers until they've stood trial and are sentenced to hang."

The mayor found his tongue. "You mean you want those men to be chained to a post until they hang?"

"That's right," Clint said. "It won't be the first time I've done it this way. If you had a good, solid jail, now that would make a difference. But seeing as how you don't, being chained and watched by the whole damn town is about the most sure-fire way I can think to make sure they don't escape. Oh yeah, don't feed them much, and keep them thirsty as well."

"But . . . but that's cruel!" the mayor blurted.

Clint wearily dismounted and took a fistful of the

mayor's starched shirt. "When they robbed the bank and killed four brave townspeople, what was that?"

Judging from the angry comments of the townspeople, Clint had won his argument. And when he dismounted, someone took his horse and led it away as if it were a prized animal. A few people even tried to pull hairs from Duke's coat for souvenirs.

Mayor Perkins cleared his throat. "I'm afraid we have another problem."

"What's that?"

"No courthouse."

"Well, how does the judge hold court?"

Perkins shrugged. "To begin with, Judge Fergus Cotter only rides through on Tuesdays. And then we usually just have a few misdemeanors for him to adjudicate, and he takes care of them in the barber shop. But this will be a murder trial!"

"Then we'll hold it right here in the street for all the people to watch," the Gunsmith said, studying the people around him. "I think what the citizenry of Candelaria needs is to see justice in action. Maybe it would give some of them the spine to stand up and fight against the likes of the Pike brothers."

The mayor blustered, "This is a good town, sir!"

"It has room for improvement," Clint said. "And when Tuesday rolls around, I think we're going to see that justice is swift."

Mayor Perkins did not look too pleased. "I think it would be much better if we hired you to escort our prisoners to Carson City, where they could be tried, sentenced, and hanged at the Territorial Prison. All this business of a trial and everything . . . well, many of these people have suffered at the hands of these brothers, and I'm sure they'd rather just put the entire episode right out of their minds."

Clint had heard this same refrain many times in many

different towns. People did not like to be reminded that life on the frontier was often without law and justice. That the strong often prevailed over the weak simply because of their strength. That right or wrong did not matter, only who could draw his gun fastest and hit what he aimed to hit.

"You're going to have a trial," the Gunsmith said, his voice taking on a hard, uncompromising edge. "I won't transport these men to Carson City so you can have your dirty wash laundered elsewhere. Is that understood?"

The mayor nodded. He glanced over at the Pike brothers and said, "Just don't be surprised if you have a hell of a time finding a jury."

"Why should that be a problem?"

"It just will be," the mayor said stubbornly.

Clint looked to Ruth, whose husband had been killed by the Pikes. "Will you serve?"

She nodded her head.

Clint looked over at Molly Malloy and Heck Jacobs. Molly had also lost her husband to the Pikes, and Jacobs had lost his cousin. "Will you serve on a jury that will hang these three men?"

"Damn right! Jacobs bellowed.

"So will I," Molly called.

The mayor scowled. "I'm sure that they are a little prejudiced against the Pike brothers. They are not exactly impartial."

"They'll do," Clint said. "And you can be sure that I'll find a few others to join them tomorrow when the trial starts. Now, I'm tired, dirty, thirsty, and hungry. So why don't you appoint some of your brave citizens to guard these three, while a few more find a post and sink it deep?"

Before the mayor could argue that he had no authority to order anyone to do anything, Clint was moving off through the crowd.

THIRTEEN

Judge Fergus Cotter was a tall, gangling red-head with a mustache and a wispy voice. But his eyes had a piercing quality, and he had a no-nonsense approach to justice that had earned him respect in every town where he was expected to deliver justice. The man was in his early fifties, taciturn by nature, and ill disposed toward frivolity or small talk.

"So," he said, studing the three Pike brothers chained to a huge post in the street before returning his attention to Clint. "You are the famous Gunsmith, and I'm supposed to select a jury. What are they charged with?"

With most of the town leaning forward to overhear, Clint related how the Pike brothers had robbed the bank and the Wells Fargo office, killing four people. He finished by saying, "The Wells Fargo manager, Mr. Eubanks, also lost his life trying to apprehend these outlaws."

"Killed by which man?"

"He was killed by an Indian."

"And where is he?"

"I killed him. Mr. Heck Jacobs, our blacksmith saw it happen. It was a fair fight. I stabbed the Indian to death with his own knife in self-defense."

"All right. Let's begin by selecting a jury."

The judge stood up on the edge of a water trough and, balanced there, he began pointing at people in the crowd and saying, "You, you, you, you. And you, you, and you. That ought to do it. Now, come over here and let's get this trial under way."

Clint watched the seven men the judge had selected come forward. None of them looked happy. Four were obviously miners, one was a freighter, and the other two were shop owners. It was a good cross-section of the mining town's population.

"Now," the judge said, when the seven men had lined up, "I begin by swearing you all to uphold your duty as. . . ."

One of the seven blurted, "Judge? Judge, sir?"

Fergus Cotter hated to be interrupted in mid-sentence, partly because he often lost his train of thought. "What!"

"Well, sir," the miner said, twisting his cap in his big, callused hands. "I got a wife and three children, and I'd just rather not be on this jury."

"Me, neither," said one of the storekeepers. "I've also got a bunch of kids and. . . ."

Cotter's face, red normally, went almost purple. "What in blazes has having a family got to do with being on my jury or not!"

The storekeeper swallowed noisily. "Well, what happens if they escaped or someone got loose before they was hanged? I figure, the way they think, they'd come right after me if I came up with a hanging sentence."

"I figure the same," another of the men chosen for jury duty complained as the others echoed his sentiments.

Cotter had such a fit that he nearly lost his balance and fell into the water trough. "Why, you gutless bunch of cowards! How is justice ever to prevail out in the West if men haven't the backbone to stand up and be counted?"

He glared at the seven. "Now, all you men are going to be jurors, and you'll do your duty or, so help me God, I'll send you to the State Penitentiary in Carson City."

No one asked on what grounds they could be sent to prison because, from the look of Judge Cotter, they were sure he'd think of something.

"All right, then," the judge said, shaking as if to rid himself of their objections. "Enough of this nonsense. Let's get me a table and chair and some more chairs for the jury. This court will be in session in one hour."

Mayor Perkins jumped to do the judge's orders, and so did a lot of others. Clint beamed, because Fergus Cotter was exactly the kind of judge that the West so desperately needed. He was a man of action.

"What are you grinning about?" Cotter snapped.

"Not a thing," Clint said. "I just like to see a man well suited to his chosen profession."

For the first time since his arrival, Cotter allowed himself the thinnest smile. "When this is trial is over, I expect you to have dinner with me. We'll have some tall tales to tell."

"You're on," Clint said. "And I'm glad you don't expect the trial to drag on very long."

"What's to drag on? The whole town saw them rob the bank and shoot their fellow citizens, didn't they?"

"Yes."

"Well," the judge said, stepping down from the water trough and reaching inside his coat pocket for a small, silver flask of whiskey, "then I don't see why the whole

matter should take long to decide. In fact, the wonder is
that this town didn't get itself mad enough to deliver a little
rope justice."

"They're mighty afraid of the Pike brothers," Clint said.

The judge looked at the three sullen and haggard men
chained to the post. "They hardly appear dangerous anymore. In fact, they look like they've gone through hell."

Clint chuckled. "That's because I made them hike out of
Death Valley. They're footsore and plain worn out. Makes
them a little easier to handle."

Judge Cotter chuckled. "You should not have given up
your badge, because you also are a man who does his job
very well. With that in mind, will you be the bailiff and
make sure the crowd, or the prisoners, does not become
unruly?"

"Be glad to."

"Excellent," the judge said. "Now, while I retire to my
hotel room to freshen up, please make sure that everything
is in order for the trial to begin in one hour."

An hour later, everything was ready. The three Pike
brothers were still chained to the huge post, and because
Clint did not trust them with chairs, they would either have
to stand, or squat in the dirt.

Judge Cotter was seated behind a table, and the jury that
he selected also had chairs. Clint had made sure that the
jury sat facing away from the Pike brothers, who glared
with such malevolence that they would have intimidated all
but the bravest of men.

When the judge gave Clint the nod, the Gunsmith stood
up and said, "Hear ye, hear ye, this court is now in session, the Honorable Judge Fergus Cotter presiding!"

The judge banged his gavel on the table, and all talk
died. Cotter looked over the crowd, and then he spoke to
the jury. "Gentlemen, you are charged with a sacred re-

sponsibility this day. One that juries have undertaken and carried with honor since the beginnings of civilized man. What you are charged to do is to determine if the defendants are innocent or guilty. That is *your* part. *My* responsibility is to deliver, unflinchingly, a proper and just sentence that will fit the crime. Are there any questions?"

Not one of the jurymen moved a muscle.

"Very good," Judge Cotter said. "Let us begin with a testimony by someone who actually saw the Pikes enter the bank and the Wells Fargo office, and then saw them gun down four citizens, while making good their bloody escape."

An older man stood up. "My name is Tom Benson," he said. "I drive coaches for the Wells Fargo company. I was in the office when Jud and Ulysses Pike came inside. Jud near killed me and Mr. Eubanks on the spot. When they raced out the door and the shooting started, I saw Ulysses gun down two of the dead men. Saw 'em just as plain as day."

"Very good, Mr. Benson. Now, let's hear from someone else. How about the bank manager?"

The bank manager also testified, because everyone was watching and he had no choice. "Mitch and Hank came into the bank and ordered everyone except me to get down on the floor and close their eyes. I had just opened the safe at eleven o'clock, and there was nothing I could do but watch helplessly as my depositors' money was stuffed into saddlebags. Mitch warned that if we made a sound before they left, he'd come back and kill us all."

"I'll kill you anyway!" Mitch shouted from where he was chained. "Me and my brothers will kill the whole damn jury if they sentence us to hang. And the same goes for anyone who testifies against us!"

The bank manager paled. His mouth worked silently,

and then he clamped his jaw shut and said, "I believe I have said enough."

Judge Cotter was furious. "This jury will not be intimidated by the defendants!"

"How are you gonna stop us?" Ulysses demanded.

The judge had an answer. "Gunsmith, silence the prisoners. Silence them in any way necessary, including a bullet."

Clint drew his gun, and as the crowd separated, he cocked the hammer. When he came up to Mitch, he said, "If you don't want a bullet in your brain, I suggest you keep quiet."

"When this is over and we are free, you're also on the list."

Clint didn't see much to be gained in pointing out the obvious fact that he was not too concerned about their threat.

Judge Cotter called for other witnesses from the crowd, but no one volunteered except Heck Jacobs, Ruth, and Molly. When they had finished their testimony, the judge said, "Isn't there anyone else out there willing to testify?"

No one moved.

The judge shook with fury, but managed to control his temper enough to snap, "I command the jury to reach a unanimous verdict and, given the eyewitness accounts we have heard, I see no reason to disband for a deliberation. Jury, accept your commission and arrive at a verdict now."

The jury fidgeted and squirmed in silence until the judge jumped out of his chair and said, "I'm calling a five-minute recess so that I might confer with the jury."

He banged his gavel and called the jury members up to his table. Clint did not hear all that Judge Cotter said, but he knew there was heat in the man's words, and when he had finished speaking, the jury was grim. They returned to their chairs and the judge said, "Now may I have your verdict."

"Guilty of murder." "Guilty." "Guilty." "Guilty as charged."

The judge relaxed and said, "It appears that we have a unanimous verdict of guilty in murdering four townspeople and robbing the bank and the Wells Fargo office. The sentence for these crimes is that the defendants shall be hanged at the Territorial Prison in Carson City by the necks until dead. This court is now adjourned."

He banged his gavel, and everyone started talking at once until Mitch and Ulysses began to shout, "We're coming back, and we'll make an example of every man on the jury, and then we'll start with the ones who testified!"

Cotter motioned the Gunsmith forward. "After we have dinner tonight, I want you to take those animals to Carson City to be hanged."

"But I've no authority. . . ."

"I give you the authority by appointing you a Federal Marshal," Cotter said, taking a badge out of his coat pocket and pinning it on Clint's chest. "You're the only one who can possibly do the job. Everyone else is afraid. You *have* to do this, Gunsmith."

"All right," Clint said, thinking about how he had been planning to rest and visit Ruth later on, so that they could get intimately acquainted. "All right, I'll do it."

"Splendid!" the judge said. "This will give you just enough time to make your preparations for leaving. I will see you for dinner."

Clint nodded. He looked over at the Pike brothers and listened to them again threatening the jury and the crowd. He knew that getting the Pike brothers to Carson City was going to be a nasty assignment.

FOURTEEN

Heck Jacobs, his shoulder still heavily bandaged, stood before the Gunsmith and toed the dirt as Clint led Duke out of his stall and prepared to leave. He was troubled and said, "You're going to need someone to help you deliver the Pike brothers to Carson City. I want to be the man."

"Uh-uh," Clint said, currying the dust from his horse's coat and then reaching for his saddle blanket. "You're in no shape to travel. Hurt the way you are, I'd wind up having four people to worry about instead of three."

"But the Pikes will try to kill you and escape! There's just no way that they'll allow you to get them to a hangman's noose at the territorial prison."

"I know that," Clint said, whipping his saddle up on the blanket and reaching for his latigo and cinch. "But you saw what an easy time I had bringing them up from Death Valley."

Heck was surprised. "Are you planning to neck-rope and march 'em all the way up to Carson City?"

"Maybe." Clint finished tightening his cinch. "One thing sure, that's the way they'll start out."

"I don't think they're men enough to make that walk. Not in this heat. And water is scarce between here and the Walker River. You aren't taking but one goatskin bag."

"I've been up the road north out of here before, and I know where there's water."

Clint shook the big blacksmith's hand. "Thanks for boarding my horse and making sure his shoes are set tight."

"I just wish I could go along," Jacobs said. "The idea of you and the three of them sure doesn't give me an easy feeling in the gut."

Ruth stepped into the barn, overhearing Jacobs' reservations. "I couldn't put it any better," she added. "Clint, isn't there anyone who will go along with you?"

"Sure, Heck has volunteered. But I figure this is one job I'm going to have to do alone. You don't hire just anyone off the street to do this kind of work. It's got to be someone who knows what they're doing when it comes to transporting dangerous men; they have to be constantly on the alert. A greenhorn will make big problems every time." Clint grinned. "Cheer up! I've taken worse men to the gallows before."

"That's hard to believe," Jacobs said. He looked at Ruth, and then he headed for the door, saying, "I'll get them unhitched from the post and lined up and ready for you."

"Thanks," Clint said.

When he and Ruth were alone, Clint took the woman in his arms and said, "Stop worrying. It's less than two hundred miles to Carson City, and I'll be back in a couple of weeks. Maybe sooner."

"You won't go on without me?"

"Nope." Clint winked, kissed the woman, and then mounted his horse. "I'll come back for you. Just have that house of yours sold and your money all ready to spend."

"You don't mean that, do you?"

"Naw," he said. "But I've only got a couple hundred dollars. If you match that, I'll take you over to San Francisco and show you the wildest spots on the Barbary Coast. We can have some real good times."

She looked up at him with expectancy. "I'll be packed, have my money in hand, and be ready. Are you sure you and I can't take just an hour or two to climb up in the hayloft and have some fun?"

Clint laughed. "You're a brazen woman! But the truth is, I need all the strength I've got for the days ahead. So I'll just put a hold on your offer until I come back."

Clint rode through the door and up the street. A large crowd parted for him until he reached the post, where Jacobs had already unlocked the three convicted killers. Clint knew something was wrong when he saw that all three brothers were grinning from ear to ear.

"Clint," Jacobs said, "there's been a change in plans."

"What's that supposed to mean?" Clint asked, following Jacob's eyes to the Wells Fargo stage, which was hitched and ready to roll.

Judge Cotter came bustling through the crowd, and when he spotted Clint, he came over and said, "I know you think that the way to get those three men to Carson City is to make them march, but I can't let you do that. In this heat, with few water holes, and in their present physical condition, the prisoners would never make it. That's why I've busied myself sending telegrams to Wells Fargo, and they've agreed to donate the use of this special coach to transport the Pike brothers to Carson City. You see, they have as much at stake in seeing these outlaws hang as we do."

Clint did not like surprises, and he did not appreciate other people interfering with his plans. "I'd as soon do without the coach."

"I know that. But like I said, I have a responsibility to see that these three men arrive safely in Carson City in order to receive justice at the end of a rope. That's why I'm coming along."

Clint looked up at the driver, who tipped his hat in greeting. Clint returned his attention to the judge. "Do you know how to use a gun? Because if something goes wrong, and you don't, I won't be able to protect you."

"I carry a gun, and I know how to use it," Cotter said.

Clint knew when he was beaten. "All right," he said. "But if the Pikes are going to ride, then they'll do it chained to the roof of the coach. It's too damn cozy down inside for my comfort. Agreed?"

"You're the one in charge," Cotter said.

"All right then," Clint said, drawing his six-gun and using it to motion to Jacobs that the three prisoners should be brought up on the roof and chained securely. "Heck, chain them hand and foot. Don't give them any slack at all."

The blacksmith nodded, and as Clint held his gun on the brothers, he watched carefully until he was satisfied that the prisoners were chained securely.

Ulysses Pike shook his chained fist at the townspeople. "We'll be back soon!" he roared. "And every man on the jury is going to die! And every man—and woman—who testified against us is going to wish they had never been born!"

Ulysses was looking at Ruth and Molly when he made his threat, but every juryman also shivered.

Mitch laughed, and big Hank showed his teeth and then also shook his manacles and cursed the crowd.

Clint wanted to get out of this town before the Pike brothers instilled any more fear, but there was one more thing that had to be taken care of first, "Driver, I'll be riding my horse alongside the coach so I can watch them every minute. Do you have any weapons up there?"

"Just my sidearm. No shotgun."

"Toss your sidearm down to me," Clint ordered. "If you're unarmed, then I don't need to worry about one of those killers grabbing your gun and using it on us."

"But. . . ."

"Driver, do as he says!" Cotter shouted from inside the coach.

The driver unholstered his six-gun and tossed it to the Gunsmith, who shoved it into his saddlebags. That done, he said, "Let's roll!"

The driver cracked his whip, and with the Pike brothers ranting and cursing, the coach rolled out of town. Clint heard men and women shouting his name, but he paid them no mind. He positioned himself just off the rear wheel of the stage, where he could keep an eye on the Pike brothers without being swallowed up in the dust.

When they reached the open country and started north, the Gunsmith finally had a chance to assess what lay in store. In a way, he was glad that the judge had gotten a stagecoach. Instead of taking a week to reach Carson City, now it would take less than three days. He'd stay in Carson City two days to rest and make sure that the brothers were hanged, then he'd start back. With luck, a week later he'd be making love to Ruth Eubanks under some pine tree way up in the cool, cool Sierras.

FIFTEEN

The first day and night out of Candelaria, they covered nearly eighty miles and changed teams of stage horses four times. The second day seemed even hotter than the first, and by nightfall they were better than halfway to Carson City, but Clint knew that he could not go on or push Duke another full day without resting for the night.

Coyote Station wasn't much, but Clint knew it would have to do. It was nearly sundown when the stage station loomed up out of the flat desert country. The only good thing about Coyote Station was that it had a cold-water spring and a big stand of cottonwoods that gave welcome shade. Other than that, all Clint could see were pole corrals in bad need of repair, a small, crumbling rock house with a rusty tin roof, a brush-covered lean-to where the blacksmithing work was done, and a ten-by-ten combination bunkhouse and cookshack, where the operator of the station cooked meals for himself as well as the passengers.

"It'll have to do," Clint said, wearily unsaddling Duke. He watered and grained the animal heavily before turning the weary gelding out among the team horses.

"What about the prisoners?" Judge Cotter asked. "How do you propose to keep an eye on them?"

Clint looked around. "You see that first big cottonwood tree?"

"Yes."

"I'm going to chain them to it right after they relieve themselves and get some food. That's where they'll sleep, and if scorpions or a rattlesnake comes calling in the night, then it'll be interesting to see who poisons who first."

Cotter chuckled. "You are a hard man, Gunsmith. But I can't say I mind that at all. In my work, what I see year after year are the strong killing and taking advantage of the weak. I'm afraid the only thing men such as the Pike brothers understand is force. Wherever their kind discovers weakness, they feed like parasites."

Clint removed his sweat-stained hat. He took his handkerchief and dipped it into the water trough. He watched a big sorrel coach horse come over to Duke and nip the gelding hard. In answer, Duke spun around and planted both of his iron-shod rear hooves against the sorrel's ribs so hard that the animal staggered. Before it could recover, Duke spun around, ears flattened against his head, and took a big patch of hide out of the sorrel's neck.

The sorrel was now in full retreat, and Clint had a grin on his face. "That tells me that Duke isn't altogether worn out."

"He's a fine animal," the judge said. "When I was younger, I used to ride a horse something like that one. I had him nearly fifteen years before he grew so old and lame that I had to have him put out of his misery. Sometimes I think we are kinder with our animals than we are with humans."

"You're pretty philosophical today, Judge."

"The law is philosophical," the judge said. "It's also incredibly naive and idealistic out here in the West."

Clint agreed, and he would have enjoyed talking longer to the judge, but Hank Pike had begun to shout that he wanted down from the top of the coach. Hank's brothers were stretched out on the roof of the coach, and they looked burned to a crisp and half dead. Small wonder. Any man would look bad after two days of baking in the hot desert sun. It was not Clint's desire to torture the killers, but he had learned from hard experience that when a law man started to worry about his prisoner's welfare and comfort, he was putting his own life in serious jeopardy.

"I better get them down, fed, and watered," he said, taking out the keys and then unholstering his gun. "Driver," Clint said, "unlock the prisoners and then toss me back the keys."

The driver, a sullen, uncommunicative man in his thirties caught the keys and then unlocked the padlocks. It was easy to see that he did not want t get near the prisoners. His movements were nervous, and when Hank took a swipe at him with his manacles, Clint unleashed a bullet that sent Hank's Stetson spinning.

"One more trick like that and the next shot goes through your brain!" Clint shouted. "Either that, or maybe I'll decide to just let the three of you lay up on that roof until we reach the prison. If you're still alive when we get there, fine; if not, then you save the hangman his work."

Mitch raised his head from the roof of the coach. "You bastard," he choked. "I'm going to see you suffer before my life is over. You and the judge are both going to die. And then me and my brothers are going to make everyone in Candelaria who spoke or went against us pay, starting with the jury."

"Your thinking amazes me," Clint said. "You and your

brothers ride into that town, kill four people, and rob the bank, and you think that you deserve sweet revenge. Truth is, you deserve to hang."

"That's right," the judge said.

"Stow it, you old goat!" Ulysses choked.

The judge did not like being called an "old goat," but he let it ride, and before he went into the rock house to see what was cooking, he said to Clint, "You were right about chaining them to a tree until morning. Vermin like that deserve no kindness."

Clint motioned with his gun for the outlaws to come down from the roof of the coach.

"Hell," Mitch complained, "we're still all chained together!"

"Then one of you had better not slip and fall," Clint said.

The brothers, stiff, filled with murderous intentions, and glaring at the Gunsmith, slowly climbed down from the roof. Once they were all on the ground, Clint lined them out for the stand of cottonwood trees.

"Ain't we even gonna wash up and eat inside!" Ulysses growled.

"Nope," Clint said. "You can wash in that little stream yonder. Now hurry along. Driver, get those chains and shackles down from the roof of the coach and bring them along. I'm going to need your help."

"I didn't hire on as no damned guard," the driver complained. "I don't want no part of them."

"What you want doesn't carry any weight with me," Clint said. "So get those shackles and follow us over to that first tree!"

The driver knew better than to refuse, but it was easy to see that he was scared half to death by the brothers and, if there was any sudden trouble, he'd be next to worthless.

Clint allowed the brothers to relieve themselves, then

wash their hands and bathe their sunburned faces before he made them go over to the first big cottonwood tree. "Driver, real slow and easy, I want you to bring those chains over and shackle them back up to the tree."

The driver swallowed noisily. He started forward with the shackles, and Hank snarled at him and said, "You come near me and I'll break your goddamn neck!"

The driver froze, and his eyes widened with fear. He looked at Hank and the other two, and then he shook his head and backed away, dropping the shackles in the dirt. "I ain't going near them, dammit! You're the Gunsmith, you chain them to the damn tree!"

Before Clint could answer, the driver spun on his heels and raced away, leaving the Pike brothers to grin in triumph. Mitch shook his head and said, "Looks like you're going to have to chain us to that tree, Gunsmith. So come on and let's see how you do it."

Clint scowled. He could call the station attendant or the judge, but that would undermine his authority and make him look weak. Weakness was fatal in this line of work, so Clint pointed his gun at Mitch and said, "I'm going to count to three, and if you haven't started to pick up that chain closest to you and shackle yourself to the tree, then I'm going to blow your kneecap to pieces."

Mitch paled. "You're bluffing!"

"I don't bluff," Clint said. "Bluffing gets a law man killed once the word gets around. Nope, I've had to do it before, and I can do it again. Besides, what does it matter if you walk like a man up the gallows stairs or you crawl? Either way, one leg will get you where you're bound."

It was Clint's turn to smile now. "One . . . two. . . . "

Mitch's nerve broke about a half-second before Clint would have put a bullet through the man's kneecap. Ranting and cursing, Mitch grabbed up the chain and shackles and chained himself to the cottonwood tree.

"Now you boys follow the leader," Clint said to Hank and Ulysses. "Or, if you don't want to do as you're told, you can also see if I'm bluffing."

Ulysses and Hank were now convinced that Clint was definitely not bluffing. They also chained themselves up to the tree.

Clint stepped forward and checked to make sure that each lock was secure, then he backed out of reach and holstered his gun. "I'll bring some food out to you as soon as we've eaten," he promised.

The Pike brothers would have cursed him if they'd dared.

Inside the rock house, the air seemed much cooler. The judge was the only one who had bothered to fill Clint a plate of potatoes and jack rabbit stew. "Better sit down and eat," the judge said.

Clint ate, even though bone weariness and the heat had robbed him of his appetite. When he was finished, he and the judge filled three more plates and took them out to the prisoners, who were leaning against the tree. The brothers snatched the plates and ate like famished animals.

That evening, Clint went to check his prisoners once more before he went to his bedroll and closed his eyes. He did not awaken until morning, when he heard the sound of gunfire, and then he came out of a dead sleep like a man trying to claw his way out of a twenty-foot-deep muddy hole. And even before his hand went for his gun, he knew something was terribly, terribly wrong at Coyote Station.

SIXTEEN

Clint got tangled up in his bedroll, and it seemed to take him forever to tear himself free and jump to his feet with his gun in his hand. The first thing he realized was that it was full daylight, and the second thing was that he was alone in the bunkhouse.

Clint shook the cobwebs out of his head and almost rushed out the door, but old instincts saved him from certain death. Pressing against the door frame of the bunkhouse, he had a clear view of the station yard, and what he saw made him gnash his teeth in anger.

Ulysses Pike had a gun in his fist, and it was smoking. The stagecoach driver was lying in a pool of his own blood, and the station operator was badly wounded, dragging himself across the yard in a futile effort to reach the rock house. And finally, Judge Cotter was being half-strangled by Hank Pike, whose mighty forearm was locked around the poor judge's scrawny neck. The only saving grace was that the three men were still manacled to the big cottonwood tree, though it was clear that Ulysses had wasted at least one bullet in an attempt to shoot a padlock apart.

It was also clear that Ulysses Pike had been waiting for the Gunsmith to come rushing outside. Half asleep, Clint would not have lived long enough to reach the yard before he'd have been gunned down. Clint had spoiled the plan, but the odds were all still in favor of the Pike brothers.

"Gunsmith!" Mitch yelled. "Throw down your gun and come out with your hands high in the air!"

"Go to hell!" Clint shouted out through the doorway.

Hank lifted the judge completely off the ground and let the older man dangle and choke until his face turned completely purple. Clint swore silently and yelled, "Hank, put him down or I'll come out shooting, and you're the first one who will die!"

Hank set the judge down on his feet, but he was just smart enough to keep his heavily muscled forearm around the judge's throat and use the man as a shield.

"Come out or I'll kill the judge and the station attendant!" Mitch screamed. "You know we got nothing to lose by adding a few more to our tally."

Clint was wide awake now. He knew for certain that if the judge could speak, the man would tell him not to come out under any circumstances, because he'd be gunned down and all would be lost.

Clint took a deep breath and force himself to consider things very clearly. The station attendant looked to be mortally wounded and the driver was dead. It did not matter how the Pike brothers had managed to come into the possession of a gun and the judge. All that mattered now was that Clint somehow try to think of a way to save Judge Cotter's life and reach the station operator and see if anything could be done for his wound.

"Gunsmith! Do you hear me? Throw your gun into the yard, and come out with your hands over your head."

"Don't do it!" the judge managed to croak.

Hank tightened his grip on the judge's throat, and Clint had to endure watching the old man dance in the air until, suddenly, he went completely limp. Both Mitch and Ulysses looked at the judge, and it was Mitch who yelled, "Goddammit, Hank! I told you not to kill him yet!"

"He ain't dead!" Hank said, kneeling and holding the judge up before him. "He just passed out."

Clint hoped that was the case. He had really admired Judge Cotter, and the West needed more of his kind. But if the judge was dead of asphyxiation or a broken neck, then Clint figured he was going to settle the score and shoot the Pike brothers down in their chains. After all, he wasn't a law man anymore and he wasn't sworn to deliver condemned prisoners to a hangman.

"He's dead, isn't he?" Clint shouted.

The three brothers understood the implications very clearly. Ulysses was as good a man with a gun as they'd ever seen, but the Gunsmith was a legend. Furthermore, they were shackled and easy targets while Clint was free and mobile. With the judge's collapse, suddenly the odds had shifted and were no longer in their favor.

"He's breathing!" Hank bellowed. "You can see that he's breathing, can't you?"

"No," Clint said. "I sure can't. Throw down the gun, Ulysses. It's over."

Mitch backed up to the tree and inched around behind it until he was half hidden. Hank dragged the judge around, and Ulysses was the last one to follow. "You want us, come and get us!" Ulysses bellowed.

Since there was no back door or even window to the rock house, Clint knew that he had no choice but to go out the front with his gun bucking in his fist. Taking a deep breath, he dashed outside, threw himself sideways, and rolled as bullets bit into the rock wall. Clint unleashed two bullets in the general direction of the Pike brothers for no other reason than to keep them honest, and then he sprinted for the cover of the rock house. Three bullets stitched the air around Clint before he hurled his body through the doorway and scrambled out of Ulysses' line of fire.

Clint tried to think how many shots Ulysses had fired. At least five. Maybe six! The fool might be out of bullets! Minutes passed, and just about the time that Clint's hope was rising, and he was sure that Ulysses was packing an empty gun, two gunshots told him otherwise. Clint peeked around the corner of the rock wall to see that Ulysses had just shot his chain apart and was free. Even more disheartening was the sight of Ulysses with a gunbelt filled with bullets. The man reloaded and then emptied his gun once more as he shot the chains that held his brothers away. Reloading a third time, Ulysses now turned his undivided attention on the Gunsmith.

"Gunsmith!" Ulysses yelled as he finished reloading. "You've lost, and the game is up! So why don't you come out and face me like a man before I shoot the judge to death!"

Clint looked around the room, desperately hoping that he could see a shotgun or even another gun. He was down to just four bullets, and the odds had swung back against him. Up on his feet, Clint made a quick search of the room and found nothing but an old percussion rifle. He found powder and balls, but not caps, and so the rifle was useless.

"I'm counting to three!" Mitch yelled. "You remember how you were going to blow our kneecaps off at the count of three? Well, this time we're going to kill the judge. He's still alive. Look outside and you can see that I'm telling the truth."

Clint looked outside and, sure enough, Judge Cotter was sitting up, dazed but very much alive. Hank still had his arm around the man's throat, but he wasn't putting any pressure in the hold.

"All right!" Clint shouted. "It's you and me, Ulysses. Step out in the open, and we'll find out who's the best."

Clint emerged from the doorway, his gun still in his fist, but held at arm's length at the side of his leg. Ulysses, tall, sunburned, and deadly, stepped apart from the others after whispering something that Clint could not hear. Manacles and broken chains were still attached to Ulysses' left wrist and ankle, but his right hand gripped a fully-loaded six-gun, and Clint knew that he had never faced a more desperate man.

Clint stopped twenty yards from Ulysses and said, "It's the end of the line for you."

Ulysses thought otherwise. The gun in his fist snapped up and he fired in one smooth motion. His first bullet struck Clint in the leg, and the Gunsmith staggered before his own pistol bucked twice. Ulysses seemed to straighten even as he fired a second shot and then a third. Clint felt a bullet crease his cheek, and then he fired again and again, watching Ulysses goose-step backward into the cottonwood tree, dead on his feet.

Mitch jumped out and grabbed the gun from Ulysses' lifeless hand, and as his brother sagged down the trunk of the tree with two bullets in his chest, Mitch opened fire, and he was plenty good with a six-gun. Clint felt the impact of another bullet strike him in the side, and yet he managed to steady himself and take dead aim on Mitch. But when he raised his pistol and pulled the trigger, the hammer struck an empty cartridge.

Staring at Mitch and his own death, the Gunsmith did the only thing that he could do to save himself, and maybe even the judge. He turned and ran for his life as Mitch fired, missed, and began to reload his own empty gun.

Clint had enough presence of mind to realize that his only chance lay in reaching a deep, brush-choked *arroyo* behind the station. If he could do that, he might have a chance at hiding in the brush until the Pike brothers gave up their search.

But the Gunsmith's wounded leg and the pain in his side were slowing him down. He could hear Mitch's pounding footsteps and knew that he would not be able to reach the *arroyo* in time. So he did the only thing that he could think of, and that was to run for his horse. Angling toward the horse corral, the other horses all stampeded because they could smell his blood. Duke came trotting up as the Gunsmith tore the sliding pole gate open; and then managed to hop up on a rail. The gelding bolted through the now opened gate just as his master leaped on his back. Clint grabbed Duke's mane and held on for his life, hearing Mitch's gun banging somewhere behind him. He let the gelding race across the station yard and then down the south road until he was out of pistol range and then even out of sight.

"Whoa," Clint whispered. "Whoa, boy!"

The gelding slowed to a walk, and then stopped completely. Clint unbuttoned his shirt and then used his teeth to tear it into strips. The wound at his sides was messy, but not deep. The bullet in his thigh was another matter, because it was still buried inside of him and it had to come out soon. Clint bound both wounds and wished like hell he could have dismounted and closed his eyes and rested. But the sun was already burning hot, and he knew that Mitch and Hank would be catching horses and coming after him, and that if he dismounted now, he would not have the strength to climb back onto his horse. Mitch and Hank would find him lying in the road, and they'd kill him for certain.

Pressing his face against Duke's neck, Clint tried to stop the world from taking a slow spin. He knew that he was a hell of a long way from help, and that there was only one waterhole in this whole country, and that he needed water in order to survive.

"Coyote Station," he muttered. "It's my only chance. And maybe the judge is still alive."

But even as he said those words, he heard two faint gunshots coming from Coyote Station. Clint clenched Duke's mane in his fist, knowing that the judge was dead. Now it was just him against the Pike brothers, and his only chance was to double back and reach the station and its water. If he could do that, and the Pike brothers did not return, maybe he could survive until the next stage passed through this hellish country.

Maybe, but he wouldn't have bet money on it. With his empty gun, he tapped Duke lightly on the neck, and the animal responded as if he had been reined. Duke left the lonely stage road and headed into the desert. Clint hung on with the last of his ebbing strength. He rode until he began to get dizzy, and then he tapped Duke back toward the north, saying a little prayer that the Pike brothers would already be leaving Coyote Station and coming after him. If he could just get back to the bunkhouse and retrieve his gun belt, he'd be plenty willing to face both men.

All I want, he thought, is just a fighting chance.

SEVENTEEN

Clint did not remember the long journey back to Coyote Station. It might have taken one hour—or four. All he knew was that when he slid off Duke's back, he landed beside the rock house, and it was very, very quiet. He crawled into the house and lay panting in the shade, gasping as though he had run a long race. Soon he closed his eyes, and sleep came to him like a heavy blanket of darkness.

When he awoke, his head was clear, and the pain in both his leg and his side was sharp and throbbing. Clint pushed himself to his hands and knees and searched the room for his gunbelt. It was gone, just as he'd feared. He forced himself to his feet and hobbled outside to find that dusk was settling on the land. He hobbled across the station yard and knelt at the judge's side, then swore in rage to discover that the man had been executed with two bullets.

The sullen stagecoach driver was also dead, but that was not a surprise. What was surprising was that the station attendant, an old man with a shock of unruly gray hair and red suspenders, was still very much alive. He had been shot in the back of the head, but the bullet had ricocheted off his skull. He was lying facedown, so Clint rolled him over onto his back and then went hobbling off to the spring, where he found a metal dipper. Filling it with cold water. he drank his fill and then carried more back to the stage operator.

"Come on, old fella," he said, propping the man up and forcing his mouth open to pour water down his throat.

The old stock tender, a man whose name Clint remembered as Turk, roused and swallowed, then grabbed the dipper and slopped it all over his face. He opened his eyes and looked at Clint, who must have looked like hell himself, because the old man wheezed, "If we're going to die, there's whiskey buried under my bed. Might as well cash it in drunk as sober."

"You're not going to die, and you're not going to get drunk until you help me dig a bullet out of my leg," Clint said.

Turk stared up at him. "Jeezus," he whined. "I'm shot half to death, blood all over me, and I'm supposed to play doctor? The hell with that noise!"

"Help me or I'll pour all your damned whiskey out."

"Ya can't be serious!" Turk's old face reflected horror.

"I don't bluff."

"Yeah, yeah, that's what I dimly recall you tellin' them Pike brothers."

Clint pointed to Ulysses, whose body his brothers had not even taken the time to bury. "There's the proof of my words," Clint said.

Turk managed to swallow drily, and then he said, "Help me up, and let's see if we can get that damned bullet out of your leg so's we can get drunk and try to think of something good to say about ourselves."

Clint stood up and helped Turk to his feet, though it took some painful effort. "We're a sorry damn pair," he said.

"Maybe so, but we're alive," Turk replied. "And that's got to be worth something."

They hobbled and weaved their way to the rock house. Turk pulled up the floorboards and pulled out a bottle of whiskey for himself and one for Clint. "Best have a few long pulls while I boil some water and tear up some bandages."

"You ever dug a bullet out of a man's leg?"

"Nope. Dug shot out of a fella's ass that I ventilated when he tried to steal my chickens. But I don't guess that was the same. Nobody is going to bleed to death with a butt-wound, will they?"

"I don't know," Clint said. "I never shot anyone there before. Before we get started, I got to say that if I pass out or bleed to death, I want you to bury those men and put Judge Cotter in deep. He was damn good man."

"I know that," Turk snapped. "He traveled through here on his circuit for more than ten years. Kind of a stand-off-fish sonofabitch until he decided if he liked you or not. But once he decided that you weren't going to steal his wallet or step on his toes, he was a good man. Could talk for hours and hours about the law. Bored the hell out of me, and I never understood half of what he was talking about, but it sounded real elegant."

Clint dug for his pocketknife and used it to cut away a big patch of his pants so that he could get a clear view of the bullet wound. It was nasty-looking, but he knew that it had not struck the bone or a big artery. In that respect, he was lucky to be alive.

He took a long pull on the whiskey, which was better

tasting than he'd expected, and watched as Turk got the water to boiling, the bandages torn, and began to sharpen a big, rusty butcher knife with a broken handle.

"Now wait a damn minute," Clint said. "I sure as the devil ain't going to let you use that!"

"It's my best knife!"

Clint handed the man his pocketknife, which had a three-inch blade. "Use this. It's already sharp."

Turk took the pocketknife and viewed it with distaste. He sloshed a little of his precious whiskey on the wound and said, "Grab ahold of the table, mister. I figure to work fast. What about that wound in your side?"

"It's just a flesh wound," Clint said. "Nothing more than what you got across the back of your head."

"Maybe I should still look at it."

"No," Clint said decisively. "Just get the bullet out of my leg." He gripped the sides of the table and steeled himself for the pain.

Turk took one more long pull on his bottle, and then he went to work. Despite his words and his thick, work-scarred, arthritic old fingers with their knobby joints, he was skillful. All his life he had braided leather-and-horse-hair reins, bridles, and ropes, and he had a dexterity that was surprising.

Clint's own hands went white as he squeezed the table, and he clenched his teeth as the old man probed the bullet hole until he finally managed to pop the lead slug up and out of the wound. Clint heard the slug bounce off the wooden floor, and then he sagged with relief. He felt whiskey sting the newly opened wound and he grunted with pain, and then the old station operator bound up the wound tightly.

"Gonna bleed for a little while," Turk said. "You better stay off your feet."

"I can't let those dead men lie out there all night. Coyotes might decide to eat on them."

"I'll bury 'em myself," Turk said. "You go over to my bed and lay down and sleep or drink, don't matter. You'll be better in the morning, but it's going to be a while until you're fit to travel. If you try and ride out too soon, that leg will open up and you'll bleed to death for sure."

Clint hobbled over to the bed and flopped down on his back. "If the Pike brothers come riding back, you better have a gun or a rifle for me to use. My gun is empty."

"I got that old percussion rifle, but no damn caps."

"So I discovered," Clint said. "I need bullets for my Colt."

"Used 'em all just last week shootin' rabbits."

Clint shook his head and tilted the bottle up toward the roof. "Well," he grated, "if those two bastards come riding back here, we're as good as dead men."

"You may be," Turk said, "'cause you can't run and hide. But me, I can be a mile back into the sage before they get in range."

"Thanks for the comforting thought," Clint said cynically.

Turk grinned, revealing that he was nearly toothless. "That's why I figure you might as well get drunk, 'cause you can't do a damn thing to save yourself anyway."

"You're wrong," the Gunsmith said.

Turk's bushy eyebrows lifted. "Oh?"

"I still got my pocketknife," Clint said. "And like you, I know how to use it."

Turk grinned, a line of white gums. The old man recognized that Clint had given him a compliment.

Clint took another long drink and closed his eyes. A few minutes later, he heard the metallic sound of a shovel hitting hard ground. It was rhythmic, and it put the Gunsmith to sleep.

EIGHTEEN

The next five days were the longest Clint had ever spent in his life. The Wells Fargo stage only traveled between Candelaria and Carson City once a week, and by the time it reached Coyote Station, Clint and Turk were out of food and out of sorts with each other. The toothless old man had two grating habits that had nearly driven Clint up the wall —he whistled and farted in harmony to a nameless tune that never varied by a single note. Between the old man's whistles and toots, Clint could easily understand why Turk was a man banished to a lonely job at Coyote Station; civilized men and women could not have tolerated him.

"There she comes," Turk said from the doorway. "I told you he'd be in today before noon—headin' south."

Clint's leg had not healed sufficiently to allow him to ride Duke back to Candelaria, but now he could tie the gelding to the rear of the stage and ride in comparative comfort. In Candelaria, Doc Huthman could take a professional look at the bullet wound, though Clint was sure that it was healing cleanly.

The stage rolled into Coyote Station, and there was only one passenger on board, a young man who introduced himself as Tommy Tolbert.

Clint sized Tommy up for exactly what he was—a not very successful gambler.

Tommy, after learning who the Gunsmith was, managed to work up his courage and say, "I don't suppose a man like you has much time for cards?"

"Oh," Clint replied. "I've found a time or two when poker served as a welcome diversion."

"Then maybe we could occupy time on the way to Candelaria in just such an enjoyable fashion."

Clint, whose finances were not in good shape, agreed. They played poker for the next two days. Tolbert readily understood that it would be folly to cheat, considering that Clint had borrowed six bullets from the driver, and his reputation was well known all over the territory. But cheating was always on his mind, because he discovered with great regret that the Gunsmith was a first-class gambler and a man who had a good eye for hidden cards and devices.

On the last hand, while rolling into Candelaria, Tolbert did try to pull an ace out of his sleeve, but Clint grabbed the man's wrist and said in a gentle voice that was somehow far more threatening than it should have been, "You've only lost two hundred dollars; why lose your life as well?"

Tolbert, staring across the seat at the Gunsmith, swallowed and nodded, "That's a damn good point. It's just that this last pot only has thirty dollars in it, and that's every cent I have in this world. Why, I won't even have enough pocket change to buy a square meal in this town, much less buy into a game of cards."

"That's a hell of a thing," Clint admitted, releasing the

man's wrist. "I'm going to leave you five dollars. That will feed you until you can find an honest job."

"You mean, a *manual* job?"

Clint grinned. "That's exactly what I mean. They are looking for men to work the mines down here."

"I'm no miner!" Tolbert was clearly insulted. "Hell, man, I could mess up my hands working with tools."

Clint scowled. "On second thought," he said, pocketing the entire wager, "I'm not going to leave you anything. The fact of the matter is, you don't seem nearly hungry enough to consider honest work. And from what I can see, you're not a good enough card player to be honest and win."

"You just got lucky," Tolbert snipped. "My luck will change."

"Not unless you find an honest profession," Clint said as the stage rolled to a stop in front of the Wells Fargo office. "Better give the matter some serious thought."

Tolbert was so mad he exited the off-side door without even saying a word of good-bye. Clint gingerly eased down from the coach and hobbled inside the office, where he was surprised to see Ruth Eubanks, pretty as ever, handling ticketing and packages to be mailed.

The Gunsmith idly brushed his shirt, knowing he looked like hell. He had a week's growth of beard, and he'd lost a good twenty pounds since he'd left Ruth and boarded the special stage that had been hired to transport the Pike brothers to the territorial prison in Carson City.

Ruth was busy checking in packages and taking money, so Clint stepped back outside, because he did not want to interrupt her thoughts and cause a scene in front of a bunch of strangers. He would return after the stage continued east. He limped over to Duke and untied the gelding.

"I threw your saddle and bags on that handsome gelding

of yours," the driver said. "I guess this is the end of the line for you."

"For now," Clint said. "Thanks for your help."

He managed to get a foot in the stirrup and gently swung his bad leg over the cantle, then rode Duke down the street into Heck Jacobs' livery stable, where he dismounted.

"Well, I'll be damned!" Heck said, walking inside with a pitchfork in his big hands. "I thought for sure you were dead!"

"Not quite," Clint said, wishing he did not have to tell everyone in Candelaria that two of the Pike brothers had escaped from Coyote Station and had vowed to seek revenge.

The powerful blacksmith took Clint's horse and unsaddled it. "Gunsmith," he said. "I've got some bad news for you. It's about Mitch and Hank Pike."

Clint's eyes shuttered. "Have they been here already?"

"Yeah. They came three nights ago and hunted down five of the seven men who served on the jury. They didn't use guns, so there were no shots to warn people they were even in town. They pulled those poor jury members out of their beds, and Hank killed them with his bare hands. The two who escaped death are probably halfway to Texas by now. The whole damn town is nearly crazed with fear. Especially the bank manager, who testified against the Pikes at Cotter's trial."

"Judge Cotter is also dead," Clint said. "He was murdered by the Pikes. But at least I downed Ulysses. I would have killed Hank and Mitch as well, but I ran out of bullets." Clint clenched his fists in anger. "Dammit!" he swore. "The Pikes warned they'd come back to settle accounts, but even I never imagined they'd live to carry out their murderous threats."

"Oh, they carried them out, all right," Heck said. "And

they left a note saying that the killing wasn't finished. They wrote saying that they're going to get some friends, and they're coming back for the rest of us who spoke out against them. The note said if anyone tries to stop them, they'll be killed, too."

"Over my dead body," Clint growled.

"Your body don't look too good right now," the blacksmith said.

Clint studied the man. "Do you and Molly and that little orphan girl want to go away for a while?"

"No," Heck said. "I don't worry about myself so much, but I am worried about Molly and Annie."

"Stay with them both until this is over," Clint said. "Jud and Ulysses were the wildest of the brothers, and they're dead. Hank is slow but unpredictable, and Mitch has the brains. He's also damn good with a gun. I wouldn't put it past him to use Hank some way just to get at us."

"You mean he'd sell his own brother out for revenge?"

"That's exactly what I mean." Clint headed back outside.

"Hey!" Jacobs called. "Do you think there's a chance that they went back down to that secret place they've got in Death Valley?"

"I just don't know," Clint said. "But it isn't a secret place any longer. Annie and I both know where it is, and that's why I want you to keep a close eye on the girl."

"This whole town is like a keg of black powder, ready to explode," Jacobs said. "I think if you wanted to lead a posse after the Pike brothers, most every man who owns a horse and a gun would be willing to come along."

"I'll keep that in mind," Clint said. "It's just too damn bad that they didn't feel that way when I rode into Candelaria during the bank robbery. If they had, a lot of good men would still be alive."

Heck Jacobs had nothing to say to that, and Clint left

him. He was tired and weak, and his leg still pained him mightily. He guessed what he really needed was to take it easy for a couple of days and then figure out a way to trap Mitch and Hank before they returned to Candelaria and killed again.

NINETEEN

Clint hobbled toward Doc Huthman's office, and as he walked up the street, he overheard a man say, "There goes the Gunsmith, the man who let Mitch and Hank escape to murder more good people in this town."

Cold fury stopped the Gunsmith in his tracks, and he turned to look at the man who had spoken. The fellow wasn't drunk, and he wasn't some bragging kid. He was full-grown, obviously a miner, and his eyes were cold and unforgiving. He stood among a half dozen other miners, and it was obvious that each one of them felt the same resentment toward the Gunsmith.

Clint limped angrily over to face the man who'd spoken out against him. "Where the hell were you when I called for a posse to go after the Pikes?"

"I was working in the Gray Lady Mine," the resentful miner replied.

Clint looked to the others. "Were you all working? You

must have been, because none of you was here the day that
the Pike brothers shot down four men and robbed the bank.
I know that because I asked for a posse, but not one
stepped forward to volunteer."

Several of the miners looked away in embarrassment,
and it was obvious they had been present when the Pike
brothers had ridden in to rob the bank and the Wells Fargo
office. Clint singled one of these men out and said, "I
didn't run from all four of them when they charged me
south of town. I shot Jud Pike out of the saddle, and then I
went into Death Valley after the rest of them. What did you
do?"

The man shifted uneasily on his feet. "I ain't no law
man," he said, trying to muster up the courage to meet
Clint's steady gaze. "You can tell by lookin' that none of
us is."

"No," Clint said, "you aren't. But you sure could have
gotten a horse and a gun and ridden beside me to Death
Valley. When I needed help, there were only two men in
this whole damn town volunteered. The rest of you turned
your backs on me then, and I expect you'll do it again
when I need you."

"You shouldn't have let the Pikes escape from that
stage," one of them said. "They should be dead by now."

"Yeah," Clint agreed, "they should. But the driver of
the stage disobeyed me and found a gun at one of the sta-
tions. He carried it too close to the brothers, and they
snatched it out of his holster, shot him to death, then killed
the judge and wounded me and the station tender. It was all
I could do to kill Ulysses and escape with my life, so that I
can settle the score."

The miner wiped his mouth and, still not meeting
Clint's eyes, said, "The driver who came in on the stage is
telling everyone that you ran out of Coyote Station into the
brush when the shooting started."

"Wrong," Clint corrected. "I ran after facing Ulysses and gunning him down in a stand-up battle, only to discover my six-gun was empty. Running was the only chance I had to live. That's when I ran, and anyone who claims he wouldn't have done exactly the same thing is either a damned fool or a liar."

Clint's expression was hard. "Now, I am going to get the last two Pike brothers, and when I set about to do it, I'll be looking for you boys to help. Will you come . . . or run?"

"We're miners; we don't have any horses to ride."

"Heck Jacobs has a corral full of horses. I'm sure he'll let you use them for nothing if you'll join a posse."

The miners shifted nervously, and then the one whose cutting remark had first stopped Clint said, "We don't know how to ride, and we aren't any good with guns. The only thing we know who to do good is drink, dig ore, fuck, and fist-fight."

The miners chuckled, thinking that was a damned good description of their talents and interests. But the smiles on their faces slipped badly when Clint said, "You left one thing out that you do very well."

"What's that?"

"You all know how to turn your backs, tuck your tails between your legs, and run from trouble."

The miners didn't like what Clint said, but he didn't give a damn. He stood with his legs planted wide apart and challenged them to prove he was wrong or unfair by inviting them either to take a swing at him or vow to join a posse. Instead, they drifted away.

"You were pretty hard on those men," Huthman said.

Clint turned to see the doctor, and that made him relax. "I don't understand that kind of men," he said quietly, watching the miners disappear into a saloon, but not before shooting him a look of anger and resentment.

"Me, neither," Huthman said. "But you shouldn't judge all miners in this town by that group. There's been a lot of talk since the Pike brothers returned the other night and murdered the jury. A hell of a lot of talk. And I think that when you are fit to lead a posse, you'll find there will be plenty of men willing to join you."

Clint leaned against a porch post. "That's good to hear. Trouble is, I don't know where to take a posse. Mitch and Hank might have returned to Death Valley, but that wouldn't make much sense. The worst thing I can do right now is finally to get a bunch of men and then go dashing here and there all over the territory. If I do that, I leave the town unprotected."

The doctor shrugged. "Don't ask me what to do, I'm just a glorified tooth-yanker. And right now, I think we'd better have a look at that side and leg wound."

Clint glanced over at the Wells Fargo office. He could see that it was still crowded with people, and that Ruth was busy getting packages and mail ready to send cast. "All right, let's go have a look," he said.

Once inside the doctor's examining room, Huthman removed Clint's bandages and studied his thigh. "Whoever removed that bullet did a pretty fine job," he said. "And even more importantly, you've kept it clean, so it's healing nicely."

"Ought to be," Clint said. "I kept cleaning it with whiskey."

"That will help," the doctor said. "Now let's see those ribs."

Clint removed his shirt, and he looked at himself in the mirror for the first time since leaving Candelaria. He was shocked at his own loss of weight, and his ribs showed very clearly.

"Yeah," the doctor said, "you need some good rest and plenty of home cooking."

"No time," Clint said.

"Take the time," Huthman warned. "At least a week."

"And what about the Pike brothers? Am I just supposed to sit back and wait for them to fulfill their twisted plans of revenge?"

"Why not? You said yourself that you have no idea where they went. Hell, they could be waiting in some canyon less than ten miles from here. There's nothing that would suit them better than for you and the best men in this town to go racing all the way down to Death Valley for nothing. It would leave Candelaria at their mercy."

Clint said nothing while the doctor examined his ribs, and then said, "Before I change the dressings on these wounds, you need a bath."

"I'll find one."

"Tell you what," the doctor said. "I got a Chinaman who helps me out in return for my letting him use a huge tin tub in the next room to wash laundry. I'll have him boil some hot water, and I've got plenty of medicinal soap. George Bowers, the barber, will come over here for a dollar and cut your hair and give you a shave. He owes me for some work and will be glad to lighten his debt. And finally, the clothes you are wearing are filthy. Let me go buy you some new clothes at the general store. I'll bring back the right size."

Clint frowned. "Why are you willing to do all this?"

"Because there might be some other ungrateful fools out there on the street and the next time you challenge them, they might take you up and start a fight."

"That's my worry, not yours."

"Wrong," the doctor said. "The last thing you need is to take a blow in these ribs or have that leg wound reopen. Hell, that would delay your recovery for weeks! Candelaria needs you healthy, Clint. Healthy and clear-headed enough to see that nobody else gets murdered."

Clint allowed himself a smile, then dug a wad of bills out from his pocket. "Bring on your Chinaman, your barber, and some clothes just like the ones I'm wearing now."

"Boots, too?"

Clint looked down at his worn-out black boots. "Yeah," he said. "But nothing but the best. Oh yeah, and I need a new holster and a box of ammunition."

"It'll be taken care of," the doctor promised. "Because, whether or not this town realizes it, you're the only man good enough to stop Mitch Pike and his overgrown, rat-brained brother."

Clint was led into the next room, where he undressed down to his shorts. The Chinaman appeared with a platter of steak and potatoes, and while Clint ate, and water was heated, the barber shaved him and cut his hair, without getting too much hair in his food. For the next hour, Clint enjoyed a bath, a rare cigar, and a couple of glasses of the doctor's own French cognac.

Taking the cigar out of his mouth while the Chinaman scrubbed his back, Clint said, "Doc, you're treating me like a king. I don't deserve all this."

"Sure, you do! Why, I had almost ten thousand dollars in the bank when it was hit, and I'd have lost every penny of that money if you hadn't recovered it in Death Valley."

"I saved you ten thousand dollars?"

"That's right," the doctor said proudly. "Most of it I inherited last year, but a couple thousand I saved."

"In that case," Clint said. "I guess I'll have another cigar and glass of cognac on you, and I won't expect any bill for all these services."

"It's a deal," Doc said with a wink. "But in return, I ask only one thing."

"And that is?"

The doctor's expression became wintery, and his voice

shook with anger as he chocked, "Kill Mitch and Hank! Don't just wound them so I have to work on the murdering bastards."

The doctor clasped his hands together and visibly regained his control. "I guess that kind of outburst isn't very befitting of a man who swore to uphold the Hippocratic oath taken by all doctors. But the truth of the matter is that my only daughter is married to Morris Garfield, the bank president, who testified against the Pike brothers at Judge Cotter's trial. I don't want my daughter to become a widow and my grandson to be fatherless. Now do you understand?"

"I sure do," Clint said. "But you have to understand something, too. I'll go after the Pike brothers, but I suspect they'll come after me first. I am a good man with a gun, Doc, but I don't have eyes in the back of my head and, as you can see, I bleed."

The doctor scowled. "Your point?"

"My point," Clint said, "is that the Pike brothers and whoever else they may dig up could kill me and, if that happens, somebody in Candelaria had better be willing to make a stand."

The doctor nodded. He reached down and took the bottle and found a glass for himself. "I'll make a stand," he said, tossing down a shot. "And so will Heck Jacobs and a lot of others. And we won't have to be asked by you twice."

Clint winked. "That's all I wanted to hear, Doc. But you let the younger men join a posse. You're a hell of a lot more than a glorified doctor and, when the showdown comes and the gunsmoke starts drifting away, you're going to become the most important man in Candelaria."

Doc Huthman lifted his chin, and Clint knew that the man would be ready.

TWENTY

When the Gunsmith walked out of the doctor's office, he both looked and felt like a new man. His shiny new boots squeaked softly, and the doctor had even bought him a new Stetson, black to match his boots. His six-gun was resting easy in a new holster, and his shirt and pants were of the best quality. His jowls were shiny from the barber's razor, and his shaggy hair was gone. He looked like a very successful riverboat gambler or law man, both of which he'd been at one time or another.

Clint's new appearance attracted plenty of attention. He could not hide his limp as he angled across the street, and when he entered the Wells Fargo office this time, it was empty except for Ruth, who was finishing up a blizzard of company paper-work.

"I see the stage going to El Paso has departed," he said.

Ruth was so preoccupied with her work she did not look up, but only nodded.

128

Clint moved across the office and placed his hands down on the desk where she worked and said, "Sell your house yet, or have you decided to take your late husband's job and remain in Candelaria?"

Now Ruth glanced up suddenly. "Clint!" she cried, throwing her arms around his neck and giving him a big hug. "I'd heard you were back, but I've been so busy here that I haven't had a chance to come looking for you yet."

"Just as well, because you'd probably have had a hell of a time finding me in a big laundry tub in the back of Doc Huthman's office."

He kissed her on the mouth, and she seemed to melt in his arms. When she squeezed him tightly, Clint winced with pain. "Easy on the side," he said. "I'm afraid I returned a little banged up."

"You look wonderful!" Ruth said, meaning it.

"So do you." Clint also meant it. "How come you're taking care of all this?" he asked, motioning around the office.

"I was the only one in Candelaria who knew how to do it," Ruth said. "Wells Fargo sent a telegraph asking me to take over here for as long as I could. So I accepted."

"You look happy working," he told her. "Maybe you'll stay."

"I couldn't miss that promised trip to the Sierras and the Barbary Coast," she told him. "Not for anything."

Clint thumbed back his new Stetson. "I guess you know that I've still got a big job ahead of me, trying to catch Mitch and Hank. And I'm sort of worried about you working here without protection."

Ruth touched his lips. "I've worried enough for both of us. But then I got to thinking that, if the Pike brothers were really coming, and I was one of the people they wanted dead, then they'd come looking for me at the house. So I sold the house and moved into Molly's hotel. We're rooming together."

Clint groaned. "Great."

Ruth laughed. "Ah! I see what you mean! And I suppose you and Molly. . . ."

"Yeah," Clint said. "We did."

"Hmmm, well, since I'm now a pillar in this community, and no longer simply the Wells Fargo manager's wife, I have appearances to uphold."

"What are you trying to tell me?"

"Just that I can't be seen going with you into some hotel."

"I don't like the way this is shaping up," Clint said.

Ruth looked at the clock on her wall. "I close the office in five minutes."

"And?"

She kissed him and smiled. "And there is a bed in the back room, where our stagecoach drivers sometimes sleep. And I suppose that that same bed is strong enough to hold a man *and* a woman."

Clint grinned. "Why don't you pull the shades and lock the door five minutes early?"

Ruth shook her head. "I can't. Company rules say I have to open this office at eight and close it at five o'clock sharp. Nothing short of an emergency of the first magnitude can be a sufficient excuse."

Clint kissed the woman again, then slipped his hand over her breast and said, "I think this is just such an emergency, Ruth. Now do you want to pull the shade and lock the front door, or shall I?"

Ruth swallowed and squirmed, then whispered. "According to the rules, only the manager can close the office."

Clint almost laughed out loud. Ruth sounded like she had memorized the company rule book, for hell sakes!

But he let her go, and then watched as she reached into the drawer and pulled out a big ring full of keys. She selected one, and then she marched over to the door and stepped outside. Looking both left and right, and apparently satisfying herself that no customer was attempting to make a last-minute call, Ruth stepped back inside and locked the door.

When she reached up and pulled the shades, he caught a nice look at the calves of her long, shapely legs. Once the shades were pulled, Ruth seemed to relax as she padded softly across the dim office interior to take his hand and lead him into the back room.

"There're matches and a lantern beside the table," she said, closing the door softly behind them and reaching for a bow at her neckline.

Clint was suddenly in a big hurry. He found the matches and struck two of them before he got one lit and touched it to the wick of the lantern. The room brightened suddenly, and when Clint turned around, he saw that Ruth had already dropped her dress and stood prettily in her chemise.

She kicked off her shoes and came to him. "I have been waiting for you every minute of every day and night since you left for Carson City."

Clint quickly unbuttoned his new shirt, while the woman unbuckled his gun belt and holster, then his pants. She found his manhood and shivered with expectancy, for the Gunsmith was already stiffening with desire.

Ruth finished undressing, and when she pulled Clint's stiff root out of his pants, she slipped it between her thighs and wiggled it around and around until he thought he was going to come unglued.

"What are you doing?"

"Making you feel good," she said, cupping one of her large breasts and holding it tantalizingly close to his mouth.

Clint's tongue flicked out and laved the nipple, and Ruth wiggled more as her hands slipped around his waist and shoved his pants down. She began to scratch his lean buttocks with her fingernails, and Clint felt his hips rock forward, nudging at her wetness.

He pushed Ruth up against the wall and she lifted on her toes, spreading her legs enough so that when he shoved his penis upward, he felt himself enter her smoothly.

"Oh," she groaned as Clint began to slam his big rod in and out of her so hard that the thin wall shook. "Yes, my darling!"

Clint worked her against the wall until her legs began to lose their strength, and then, still impaling her, he lifted the woman up and carried her over to the spartan bunk and fell upon her like a crazed animal. Ruth cried out in pleasure as he went even deeper, and her heels began to rake up and down against the thin straw mattress.

Clint bent his head and nibbled on one of her hard nipples until she begged him to stop. "Please, please hurry, Clint. It's been so long and . . . oh, make it come quick!"

How could he refuse a woman who needed it so badly? Clint's hard, lean body covered her round, soft one, and he forgot about his bullet wounds as he lost himself in the act of their union. Ruth's head was rolling back and forth. She moaned and whimpered and all the while her own hips were grinding against the base of his penis, eager for more. Clint held out until Ruth's control broke down and she cried out with joy as her body stiffened and went hard and her legs shivered uncontrollably.

Clint knew what that meant. Growling with pleasure, his own body responded by filling her with great spurts of his seed until he was emptied, and his hips finally stilled.

Ruth was so completely spent that she could hardly move for the next few minutes. Thinking he might have given her more pleasure than her heart and body could stand, Clint began to climb off the woman, but she clamped him tight between her legs and would her arms around his neck.

"Oh, no," she whispered, "I've finally got you exactly where I've wanted you from the first moment we met. And I'm not about to let you go now."

Clint relaxed. "I'll go as soft as warm candy inside you."

"I don't care," she said, kissing his face and even his eyelids. "I don't care, because I know how to make you hard again."

Clint chuckled. "Yeah," he said. "I'm sure you can."

A half hour later, he was hard again, and this time he took Ruth with a delicious slowness. He had pulled the cot out from the wall and she draped her legs over the sides so that her feet just managed to touch the floor. Clint, up on his elbows and slightly raised on his knees, worked Ruth until her feet began to do a tap dance on the hard wooden floor.

"This is . . . this is better than I ever dreamed it could be," she panted, her eyes rolling up and the tip of her tongue showing between her lips.

In reply, Clint played the woman like some men could a fine musical instrument. He played her until she trilled like a canary, and then he played her some more until she began to thrash and hit all her highest notes.

TWENTY-ONE

With a grim smile of satisfaction shaping his thin lips, Mitch Pike watched the three men approaching on horseback. The one in the middle was so big he was easily identifiable as Hank, but it was the other two who commanded Mitch's full attention.

While Mitch had stayed close to Candelaria and kept tabs on the comings and going of its citizens, Hank had galloped off to the mining town of Silver Peak to hire a pair of special gunmen. Silver Peak was one of the roughest towns in Nevada, and one that they had often visited after pulling a holdup. Like Candelaria, Silver Peak had no sheriff, and its mortician was prospering.

When Hank and the men he'd brought grew nearer, Mitch's smile widened. "Sonofabitch!" he said happily. "He got 'em! Graves and Folsom."

Ed Graves was a very mild-looking man in his early thirties, who would not intimidate anyone with his size or his demeanor. Everything about the man looked deceptively easy-going, and that was one of the man's biggest advantages. It was only after you lowered your guard that he struck with cold and calculating efficiency. Graves was not a gunfighter, nor had he ever claimed to be. Ed Graves took pride in calling himself a professional killer. He could use a knife as well as a gun, and his special talent was that he was very, very cunning.

Frank Folsom was a pure gunfighter. Mitch did not believe the man was quite as fast as Ulysses had been, but he was smarter. Folsom never braced a man he was not sure he had the advantage over. He was also very loyal to whoever hired him and had proven he was willing to make a stand and not run when things got difficult. Folsom, it was said, was dying of syphilis, and Mitch could see how wasted the man had become. The rumor was that a whore in El Paso had given him the disease, and that Folsom had tracked her all the way to Baltimore, Ohio, just to kill her in a most horrible fashion.

"I got the men you wanted," Hank said, reining his horse up in a cloud of dust. "Graves and Folsom figure they deserve even cuts of everything we take."

Mitch leaned hard on his saddlehorn as the two hawk-faced and expressionless men stared at him. Folsom looked like walking death. His face was skeletal, and when he spoke, his flesh moved and looked as brittle as parchment paper. It was so thin that Mitch could see the bluish blood vessels underneath. Frank Folsom had always considered himself a lady's man and had bragged that he had screwed more women in his thirty-four years than most men did in their entire lifetimes.

Well, Mitch thought, it's sure as hell obvious he screwed one too many.

Ed Graves reached for his canteen. He was hot and tired and in no mood to waste time in idle talk. "Hank said you

knew when the Wells Fargo office would send out the
weekly mining shipment. He said there was a woman in
charge. Don't seem right to me."

"Oh, it's right. I've checked it out. Did he also tell you
men that the Gunsmith is in Candelaria and that he's badly
wounded?"

"Yeah," Folsom said, pulling his lips down at the
corners. "That's what brought me. He shot my brother
about three years ago. I've been waiting to get even for a
long time."

"You'll have to get in line," Mitch said. "The Gunsmith
has killed two of our brothers, and that means I want him
first."

"You're not fast enough for the Gunsmith," Folsom said
in a contemptuous voice.

"Neither are you, and neither was Ulysses," Mitch
snapped. "So when we brace him, it had better be on *our*
terms, not his."

"I got the big advantage over him," Folsom said.

"What's that?" Mitch asked, though he suspected he
knew.

"I got nothing to lose by dying. In fact, I'd get a quick
death."

"Hank didn't ride all the way to Silver Peak to bring you
up here so you could get killed," Mitch said. "So tell me
what you stand to win."

"Besides the money? Well, I figure I got about three
months left to live, and the money could make things a
whole lot nicer. But most important, for the first time in
my life, everybody would know who Frank Folsom was if
I gunned down the Gunsmith. I'd be in history books, and
there'd probably even be songs sung about me."

Mitch didn't understand how fame could matter to a
man who would be dead, but he didn't question that it

mattered a great deal to the diseased and dying gunfighter. "What about you, Graves?"

"I'm strictly after the money. That, and I remember seeing Molly when she was just a girl you and your brothers were screwin' every chance. I wanted her then, and Hank promised me that she's even prettier now and one hell of a good-lookin' woman. Is she still in Candelaria?"

"Yeah," Mitch said. "She sure is. And the bitch testified against us in front of Judge Cotter. Her and a woman named Ruth Eubanks, whose husband was killed by Indian."

"Is Ruth a handsome woman?" Frank Folsom asked, surprising everyone because, from the looks of him, it was easy to conclude that the poor sonofabitch's pecker had already rotted away.

"She's a damned handsome woman," Mitch said cautiously. "Why?"

Folsom did not answer the question. "You fixin' to kill her, too?"

Mitch remembered how Ruth had also testified against him and his brothers. "I vowed I would, yes."

"Then I want her first," Foster said with a ghostly smile. "I hate women anymore, and I can give her something that will be worse than any death you could imagine."

Mitch felt as if his face had turned brittle when he looked at Folsom, whose evil twisted intent to infect Ruth Eubanks could not have been more obvious. And even though Mitch was not a man who tolerated weakness in himself or others, the idea of this wasted syphilitic poisoning a beautiful woman went deeply against his grain. So deeply that it surprised even himself and made him say, "The women testified against *us*, not you. They're ours to deal with."

"Then deal with them, but since I have so little time left, I deserve a few earthly pleasures before I die."

"You mean," Hank asked, staring at the wasted gunfighter, "you mean that you can still get it up?"

Mitch winced, and his hand edged toward his gun, because syphilis was known to cause crazy fits of anger. But the skeletal man began to chuckle. "Yeah," he said. "And I'll tell you something else. It's gotten bigger!"

Hank stared at the gunman's crotch and then smiled weakly. Mitch looked off toward Candelaria and then said, "We'll rest your horses a couple of hours, then ride into Candelaria just after dark."

"When are we going to take the Wells Fargo office?" Graves asked.

"I'll tell you later," Mitch said, still troubled at the thought of Frank Folsom infecting the Eubanks woman with his deadly seed. "It won't be long."

"That's good enough for me," Graves said. "Hank said it might have as much as ten thousand dollars."

"That's right," Mitch told the man, forcing himself to think about the money. "Every mine in the district funnels its payroll through that Wells Fargo office. There are guards, but never more than a few. I figure that no one will expect us to try it a second time. But we will, and this time, we'll take the gold and the woman."

"And Molly?" Graves asked. "When do I get my turn at her?"

"Tonight," Mitch said. "Just as soon as we hit town and find out if she's hiding or still in her hotel room."

Graves smiled, and his eyes burned with unconcealed lust. "I remember she was always so damned pretty. But Jud was crazy jealous if anyone but his brothers so much as looked at her. And Jud was a . . . well, a man I did not want to cross."

"Jud is dead," Mitch snapped. "And you can have

Molly, because neither me nor Hank is going to get one damned bit jealous. Ain't that right, Hank?"

The giant scrubbed his lantern jaw and stubbled beard. "Yeah, I guess so," he said. "But I'd sure like to have her again myself."

Mitch said nothing as he turned and walked away. It seemed as if everyone had suddenly gone woman-crazy. Frank Folsom, who didn't look strong enough to hump an old ewe, wanted to infect Ruth Eubanks, and both Hank and Graves wanted Molly.

Hellfire, Mitch thought. I may just let the whole bunch screw themselves to death while I ride off with the Wells Fargo payroll.

TWENTY-TWO

Molly Malloy was alone in her hotel room, reading, when she heard a commotion in the alley behind her hotel. She looked up from her book and listened intently, and when she heard nothing more, she glanced toward the adjoining room, where Annie was sleeping. A smile crossed her lips. Tonight Heck Jacobs had finally worked up enough courage to propose marriage. He had been so sure that she would refuse him because of his roughness that he had even prepared a little speech promising how he'd bathe and shave every day, take her to dinner on Saturday nights, and be a good father to Annie, whom they both adored.

Molly had not had the heart to interrupt his rehearsed argument, and she'd allowed him to run through the entire thing before she'd accepted his proposal. Heck had not quite been able to believe his good fortune. He'd stammered and stuttered, and then he'd jumped up from the table and hoisted her in his powerful arms and spun her so that she had hardly been able to breathe.

"Do you mean it? Do you really?"

"Yes," she said. "I love you, Heck. But if you don't put me down, I swear that you're going to have the breath squeezed right out of me."

He'd placed her down as carefully as if she were a china doll, and then he'd kissed her in front of the whole dining room, which caused everyone to start clapping with appreciation.

It had been a wonderful evening, and just thinking about it brought Molly a warm glow. Sure, Heck Jacobs had little polish and was not very educated, but he could read and write, and he was quite intelligent. He was, she concluded, a diamond in the rough.

Molly smoothed the hem of her nightgown and returned to her book. At least a half hour passed, and then she heard a voice that was dimly remembered. Again, she placed the book down in her lap, and she frowned, listening to the heavy footsteps in her hallway.

The clock over her bed told her that it was ten-fifteen, and since that was the hour that sensible men quit the saloons and came back to her hotel to retire, Molly did not think much of the noise. But when the footsteps halted just outside her door instead of passing by, she slowly came to her feet and then walked to the door.

"Heck?" she called softly. "Heck, I'm not decently dressed and—"

Suddenly her door splintered open as Hank Pike slammed into the room. Molly was so shocked by the appearance of Hank, and so terrified, her voice caught in her throat so that, instead of a loud scream, she could only make a small choking sound.

Mitch and two other men grabbed her and threw her to the floor before she could react, and then one of the men pulled up her nightgown and tried to force her legs apart. Molly did scream now, and someone struck her across the back of the head.

"Not here, with the door half broken off its hinges!" Mitch hissed. "I told you we got some getting even to take care of first. Now, let's get her out of here and put that damned door back on and relock it, so she's not missed by anyone until tomorrow!"

Molly felt someone wrap her body with what must have been her own blankets. She could not see anything and was nearly suffocated as she felt herself being thrown roughly over what must have been Hank's shoulder, and carried out of the room. A few minutes later, she heard the squeaking protest of the rear fire escape as she was carried down into the alley and then tossed onto a wagon bed.

"You say one word, make one sound, and I'll slice your throat," a man whose voice she didn't recognize whispered. "Be a shame to waste a nice piece like you."

Molly bit back a cry that had been forming inside. She squeezed her eyelids shut and felt hot, salty tears as she reminded herself that the important thing was that they had not found Annie in the next bedroom. Annie had already suffered so much at the hands of the terrible Pike brothers.

A man rolled in beside her, and Molly felt the wagon jerk into motion down the alley, and a few minutes later she heard the tinkle of a saloon piano and guessed she was back on the main street. She had no idea where they were taking her, or why she was not already dead. Mitch had sworn to kill her for testifying against him and his brothers.

The wagon stopped, and she felt it bounce a little as men unloaded.

"Hank, keep down and stay here with the woman. If

you see any sign of trouble, knock her in the head so she can't yell, then come running. And stay low so nobody can see your size, or it's a dead giveaway for sure."

Hank nodded with understanding as Mitch, Frank Folsom, and Ed Graves headed for the bank manager's house behind Aubry's Dry Goods Store. Hank remembered very well, as did his brother, how the bank manager had testified against them before Judge Cotter that day. Well, justice was about to be administered, and all he had to do was lay in a wagon beside a good-looking woman whose body he remembered all too well.

"You're gonna pay," he whispered. "All of us are going to make you pay before Frank Folsom takes his turn and gives you his disease."

Molly did not want to hear any of this. Her mind raced as she tried to think of some way to escape. But with the giant right beside her and the damned blanket wrapped tightly around her body, she was completely helpless. The only thing she could do was to pretend she was dead. And given the way Hank was talking, death might be the best thing that she could hope for under these grim circumstances.

Mitch led Folsom and Graves to the bank manager's house, saying, "His name is Morris Garfield. He's a rabbit, and I want to be the one that kills him."

Graves and Folsom nodded. "He live alone?"

"No. He's got a wife."

"You want her dead, too?" Graves asked.

"No," Mitch said. "Only the people who spoke out against me. But if the wife doesn't cooperate, brain her."

The two men nodded. "Maybe there will be jewelry or money in the house. Bank managers do pretty good."

Mitch frowned. "Take whatever you can find. Me, I just

want to let this town know that I'm a man of my word. I don't ever want anyone to have the nerve to testify against me again."

They moved silently up to a rear window, where they had a clear view into the kitchen. It was dark inside, but when Mitch attempted to turn the doorknob, a dog started barking loudly in the house.

"Shit!" Folsom hissed. "If they're inside, they know someone is coming for them now."

Graves drew a long, thin knife from a leather sheath attached to his belt. "Step aside," he said.

Mitch stepped aside and Graves slipped his blade into the door lock and began to twist and jiggle the mechanism. By now, the dog was going crazy, and it was just inside the door.

"That yapping sonofabitch is asking for it!" Graves swore.

"He sounds pretty big to me," said Folsom, who possessed an unreasoning childhood fear of biting dogs.

The lock turned, and Graves retracted his blade, then shoved the door open a crack. The dog was big and all teeth, it jammed its head through the narrow door opening. Graves slammed the door shut, pinning its head between the door and the jam, and then he bent over, and the next thing Mitch knew, the dog yelped and was silent.

Graves shoved the door open and stepped over the dead animal just in time to see two people with candles standing in the hallway. At the sight of the intruders, the bank manager and his wife bolted for the front door, and before anyone could stop them, they were flying across the porch and racing down the street, yelling at the top of their lungs for help.

"Dammit!" Mitch cursed. "I wanted that man's scalp!"

"It's going to have to wait," Folsom said, shoving past them and disappearing down the hallway. Graves followed and both men struck matches as they began to loot the house.

Mitch could hear shouting from the center of town, so he hurried up the hallway until he reached what appeared to be a library. And over in the corner was an old safe, which Graves and Folsom were both trying to crack.

Mitch rushed across the floor and said, "Come on, dammit, we've got to get out of here before the whole town comes to investigate!"

"I can open this thing," Graves said. "I opened one just like it over in Austin."

"There's no time! You don't even know if there's anything inside of it."

"There's only one way for him to find out," Folsom said.

Mitch hurried to the window. He looked down the street and saw that a big crowd was gathering around the banker and his wife, both of whom were gesturing toward their house. Even as he watched, more and more townspeople kept pouring into the street until it looked like there were at least a hundred, and they were armed and carrying lanterns.

"We've got to get out of here!" Mitch said.

But Graves shook his head violently. "Just a few more minutes. That's all I need!"

Mitch went back to the window, and the crowd seemed poised for action. "You ain't got a few minutes. Now, come on!"

Folsom, bending over Graves, said, "I think we'd better give it up."

"You can give it up, but not me. I tell you, I've got two of the numbers, and that only leaves two to go."

Mitch spun around and saw the crowd rushing headlong up the street like a damned cavalry charge. "They're coming for us!"

He turned and raced out into the hallway and out the back door with Folsom right behind him. But not Ed Graves. Graves was the kind of man who, once he started a thing, could not bear to quit. Besides, he reasoned, everyone had heard how cowardly the people of Candelaria had acted when the Pike brothers had ridden into their town and robbed their bank. Most likely, they'd stand around in the street jawing and working up their courage for fifteen or twenty minutes before they'd dare to rush this house.

But Graves was mistaken. He was on the fourth number when the front door crashed open and a body of men came barreling down the hallway. Graves, one hand still holding a burning candle and the other poised on the combination lock, twisted around to see four men with guns pointed at him. He dropped the candle and threw himself at the window.

Glass and guns clashed in unison, and Graves landed half in and half out of the room, his face lacerated beyond recognition by the shattered glass, and his body riddled with bullets as it lay draped over the windowsill.

Mitch and Folsom sprinted up the alley, hearing the ominous volley of gunfire erupt from the banker's house. They circled the block and skidded to a halt by the main street, where they had a clear view back at the house. There were so many people with torches held aloft that the banker's yard and house appeared to be bathed in full sunlight.

"What do you think?" Folsom wheezed, still trying to catch his breath.

"I think Graves was a fool," Mitch said, even as he saw

his brother sit up in the bed of the buckboard and then crawl over into the driver's seat and unwrap the lines from the brake.

Hank, bent over to look small, and protected by semi-darkness, turned the buckboard around in the street and drove it toward Mitch and Folsom. "Would you look at that!" Mitch said. "And who said my brother was dumb?"

"Not me."

The two men watched the buckboard and team approach them unhurriedly, and just when they thought that everything was going to work out fine, Molly, still wrapped up like a mummy, rolled off the back of the wagon and landed heavily in the street. Hank did not notice and kept driving forward.

"She's rolling out of that blanket!" Mitch hissed, looking around and not seeing any saddled horses they could use in an emergency. "If she gets out, she'll start screaming, and the whole damn town will come running.

Folsom had reached exactly the same conclusion. He sprang forward and raced up the street. Hank saw him coming and stopped the wagon, but Folsom and then Mitch passed him as if chased by the hounds of hell.

Hank twisted around and peered back the way he'd come and then he saw Molly rolling free of her blankets. Molly climbed unsteadily to her feet just as Folom and Mitch tackled her high and low before she could take a step or make a sound.

Folsom's thin arm lifted once and came down like a hammer, and Molly went still. A moment later, both men were carrying her body to the rear of the buckboard and tossing it in like a sack of grain.

"Move it!" Mitch hissed as he and the syphilitic killer jumped into the buckboard, guns drawn.

Hank had a whip, and he brought it down hard across

the haunches of the two horses. The buckboard leapt forward and bounced down the street, and no one in Candelaria even noticed, because they were still staring at the
riddled body of Ed Graves, while heartily congratulating
each other.

TWENTY-THREE

Clint and Ruth had been sound asleep in the back room of the Wells Fargo office when the burst of gunfire had split the night. Both of them awakened with a start and reached for their clothes.

"What do you think could have happened?" Ruth asked, hearing the shouts and loud pounding of feet on the boardwalk.

"I don't know, but I'll bet it isn't good," Clint said, strapping on his new holster and his gun. He pulled on his new boots, which were still too tight, and headed for the back door, calling, "It wouldn't do to have people see us come rushing out of here together. Just make sure to lock the door when I leave, because you're on Mitch Pike's list."

"I know," she said, throwing her arms around his neck and kissing his lips. "Be careful."

"Maybe it's just some drunks hoo-rahhing the town," Clint said, reaching for his hat.

But the shouting was growing louder, and Clint had a feeling in his gut that the Pike brothers had paid Candelaria a little visit. When he reached the main street, he saw that everyone was running down toward the banker's house, and Clint went along after them.

"What's all the fuss about?" he asked.

"Damned if I know!" a badly winded man gasped. "But there must be something going on!"

Clint outdistanced the man, and when he came to the banker's house, the crowd parted to let him move up to the window. Clint grabbed the dead man by the hair and pulled his head up, but he was cut nearly beyond recognition. A woman fainted, and a couple of kids stared wide-eyed and then bolted away in horror at the sight of the glass-cut face.

Clint could not hide his disappointment that this was not one one the Pike brothers. "Who is he?" Clint asked the throng.

A big man stepped forward. "It's hard to tell, but I think his name was Graves. He was a killer."

"A friend of the Pike brothers?"

The big man shrugged his shoulders and looked around as if hoping someone else would have the answer. Apparently no one did.

Clint peered in the window, and when he turned around, the banker and his wife had stepped out from the others. "They killed our dog," the banker said with bitterness. "Cut his poor throat."

"How many were there?"

"I don't know," the man said. "It was too dark to see. Three at least."

"Did you recognize Mitch or Hank?"

The couple shook their heads. "It was too dark," the

woman said, holding her wrapper tightly around her shoulders. "We heard the dog, and then saw them in the moonlight when they came through the door."

The woman's lip quivered, and she dabbed at her eyes. "Our poor, brave dog!"

Clint looked to the crowd. "Did anyone at all see the Pike brothers? And where did they go?"

"This was the only one we saw, and all we saw of him was his ass-end trying to get through the window headfirst. It was darker than pitch when he blew out the candle and hit the glass. We just opened fire."

"It's a wonder you didn't shoot each other," Clint said, then quickly added, "but it's a fine thing you did to come on the run. You have every right to be proud of yourselves."

The men of Candelaria basked in the glow of Clint's praise.

"I guess we're just lucky to have gotten out of the house alive," the banker said, still looking very badly shaken. "Next time, they'll get us for sure."

"We're ready to form a posse and follow you to hell if that's what it will take to finish them off," Heck Jacobs said, and his sentiments were echoed by almost everyone.

"Thanks," Clint said, meaning it. "I guess, if nothing else, this town has come a long way since I first arrived and realized that the bank was being held up. You people seem to have realized that the law has to have your support or it's going to come up empty. But as for a posse, well, I don't think it would do much good until I ride out and take a look to see if there are any fresh tracks that are leading into the desert. And even if there are, there's no way of telling that they belong to the Pike brothers and whoever else they might have hired."

"But we can't just sit around and wait for them to come

again some night," a miner said. "I was one of the jurors who was lucky enough to be gone when they killed the others. Well, I came back to make a stand, not to be a sitting duck."

Clint heard plenty of agreement, and he understood their displeasure. The hardest thing in the world was to wait, but even waiting was better than running in circles. "I'll ride out at first light," he said. "I know the tracks of the Pike brothers' horses, and if I see them fresh, then we'll have a trail to follow. If not . . . if not, we'll just have to bide our time and be ready when they come again."

"Maybe they won't come again," the banker said hopefully. "After all, they lost one of their gang in a very violent fashion."

"They'll come again," Clint said. "I can't tell you how I know that, I just do. I watched those brothers pretty close for nearly three days before they escaped at Coyote station. They're not the kind of men who will do the smart thing. They're too proud and too sure of themselves."

Clint saw that Ruth had slipped into the crowd, and it made him think of Molly, and how she was also on the list. He was surprised that she was not present. "Heck, why don't you go check on Molly and Annie? Tell them everything is fine and they shouldn't worry."

Heck nodded and hurried off. He was moving well again, showing no lingering ill effects of his shoulder wound.

"I'd like a couple of men with lanterns to come around the back of the house," Clint said.

At the back of the house, he knelt and studied the tracks, but it was a wasted effort; the curious townspeople had already come around to peer in the door at the banker's poor dog, leaving dozens of tracks around the back door. Clint took a lantern in his hand and walked a wide circle around the yard and out to the alley. He was looking for fresh hoofprints, but he didn't see any. The Pikes—and no one had actually seen their faces—must have left their horses somewhere else and walked to this house.

Clint was still searching for signs when he heard his name being called, and then he looked up to see Heck and the little girl running across the backyard. It only took one glance at their faces to realize that something had happened to Molly. Clint felt a cold stab of dread touch his heart.

"Is she dead?"

The little girl was almost hysterical. She was crying, and it took a moment for Heck to catch his breath. "Annie never even woke up when they broke down the door and took Molly."

The news was bad, but Clint expelled a sigh of relief; he knew they had not killed Molly. But they *had* abducted her for some sick purpose. Clint remembered Molly telling him how the Pike brothers had raped and brutalized her as a girl, and he felt a knot of cold fury ball up in his gut.

"Clint, they'd pulled the broken door tight, and even I couldn't see that it had been broken off its hinges."

The Gunsmith balled his fists. "This is a mess," he admitted. "I can't find any tracks, and Annie didn't see or hear anything. So far, we have absolutely nothing to go on."

Jacobs was almost beside himself with worry. "We can't just stand around until morning! We've got to do *something!*"

Clint walked around to the front of the house, and his appearance stopped all conversation. He did not waste time, but came right to the point and told the crowd that Molly Malloy had been kidnapped.

"What we're going to do is to circle the town and search for fresh tracks." He knelt down in the yard and smoothed

the dirt. Taking his pocket knife out, he drew a set of very
large horseshoes. "If you see these tracks, they belong to
the animal that Hank rides. His horse is half draft animal,
and must weigh fourteen hundred pounds. Its feet toe in-
ward, and there are lips on the heels. Heck, how many
other horses are bound to have feet this size with this type
of shoe?"

"Not one in ten thousand," the blacksmith whispered as
he held the little girl in his powerful arms.

Clint looked up at the circle of faces illuminated by
lanterns. "I want every one of you men to take a good long
look at this drawing and remember it before you leave and
walk around out there in the brush tonight. And don't be
afraid to pull your gun and fire once if you think you've
found somethng. I'd rather you be wrong than to pass up
this horse's tracks by mistake, leaving us with nothing."

The grim-faced men of Candelaria nodded, and some
began to measure the drawing against the width of their
splayed fingers.

"If they're out there, we'll find them," a man said.

"They have to be out there," Clint said, coming to his
feet. "We can be sure they carried Mrs. Malloy off on their
shoulders."

"We don't even know for sure that it was them," a man
said.

"Who the hell else would it be, you dumb bastard?"
someone else swore.

Before Clint could step between the men, a blow was
struck and a fight began. Clint and Heck hed to wrestle the
pair away from each other and throw them to the ground.

"Stop it!" Clint yelled. "A woman's life is on the line,
and there's no damn time for this kind of stuff."

The two men picked themselves up and dusted off their
clothes. They looked thoroughly ashamed of themselves.

"All right," Clint said, looking at the pair and then addressing everyone present. "Let's fan out."

Everyone in town went out into the brush, and from a rooftop it must have looked like a swarm of giant fireflies were moving around in the desert. The men searched, often on hands and knees, but as the hours passed, hope faded. Finally, dawn crept over the eastern horizon, and everyone straggled in, looking defeated.

Heck was the most dejected one of them all. He appeared to have aged ten years, and, seeing his haggard and distressed expression, Clint walked up and clapped him on the shoulder.

"Maybe they're still in town," he said. "We'll start a door-to-door search. We won't leave anything to chance."

"Mitch wouldn't be that dumb," Heck said. "You know what I think?"

"Yeah," Clint said. "You're thinking what I'm thinking, and that is that the Pike brothers came and left in a wagon. And if that's the case, they'd have kept to the road for at least a few miles."

"So what do we do?" Heck asked.

"We search the town and eliminate that possibility, and then we saddle our horses and ride out both north and south, hoping to find a set of wagon tracks that cut off the road and lead to nowhere."

"We're grasping at straws," Heck said with a shake of his head.

"I know that, but sometimes the straws make a haypile, and you can even get lucky enough to find a lost needle if you don't give up."

Heck Jacobs straightened. "Yeah," he said, "we can't just give up. Whatever it takes, I mean to find Molly and kill those bastards!"

"We'll find them," Clint said. "There's little doubt in

my mind about that. The question is, will we find them soon enough to help Molly?"

"We have to!" Heck said passionately.

Clint nodded and then set about forming search parties, which would cover the desolate mining town from end to end.

TWENTY-FOUR

Molly Malloy awoke feeling as if her head had been split wide open. She could feel the buckboard bouncing down the road, and she wished she could pull away the suffocating blanket that covered her head. Dimly she recalled that she had been knocked senseless, and she wondered how long she had been unconscious. Because there was no way of knowing where she was, Molly lay very still, trying to control her fears and praying for some kind of miracle that would deliver her safely from this nightmare.

It seemed like hours later that the buckboard lurched violently into the sagebrush and bounced over rocks.

"Ya!" Hank shouted, making the lines pop against the horses.

"Take it all the way up this gully," Mitch said. "I don't want this wagon to be visible from the road."

"We're doin' our best," Hank snapped.

When the wagon came to a stop, Molly felt it bounce a little as the men piled off into the sage. Someone pulled the blanket off of her, and Molly held her breath and kept her eyes closed.

"Frank, unhitch and saddle both our horses," Mitch ordered. "Hank, get your horse, and then we'll throw Molly across the back of your saddle and ride."

"Where are we going?"

"I haven't decided yet," Mitch said. "The Gunsmith knows about our place in Death Valley, so we can't go there. We want to stay close enough to Candelaria so that we can finish what we started."

"I know a place," Folsom said. "It's about twenty miles east of here. We could be there by this afternoon."

"Keep talking," Mitch said.

"It's an old silver mine that's abandoned. There's a shack and corrals. They sit way up in the hills, and there's water coming out of the ground. It's a hot springs and doesn't taste good, but it'll cool, and it won't make us or the horses sick. Ed and I used it several times, and we never seen anyone near the place except a few prospectors who pass by now and then."

Hank grinned and looked at Molly with hunger in his eyes. "Has the cabin got beds?"

"No," Folsom said. "But it beats sleeping out in the brush."

"I wasn't thinking about sleeping."

"Now, wait a minute," Folsom said. "I didn't have no grudge against anybody in Candelaria. And I didn't get a damn thing back there for riskin' my life except a woman. You promised me a woman, and now I want this one. I agreed to the other one, but since we didn't get her I'll use this one."

Hank turned to his brother. "But if he uses her, then we can't, because he's got the disease!"

Mitch saw Folsom stiffen and the color drain from his face. The gunfighter's hand moved toward his side, and Mitch knew that Hank was closer to death than he could possibly imagine.

"All right, all right," Mitch said quickly. "We agreed before we went into Candelaria that Frank would get a woman."

Hank humped up his shoulders, and he was angry. "But couldn't he at least have her *after* us?"

Mitch wondered if he could outdraw and kill Frank Folsom, and then he decided that it would be foolish even to try. "No," he said, seeing the protest in his brother's eyes. "We made a deal. Frank gets the woman, and you and I will figure out how we can go back and finish what we promised to finish."

Folsom relaxed. "Why don't you boys just forget about getting even? You saw what all those people in Candelaria did to Ed. Hell, they'd have killed the three of us along with him if we'd been stupid enough to stay there and fiddle with that damned safe."

"Ed should never have stayed with it so long."

"You got that right," Folsom said. "And I'll bet that sonofabitch was empty anyway. Who ever heard of a banker putting his money in a home safe when he had a bank of his own?"

Mitch had asked himself the same question a few times during the long buckboard ride. "I always thought Ed was smarter than that."

"He was plenty smart," Folsom said. "But his downfall was his stubbornness. It could be your downfall, too, Mitch. You're being mighty stubborn about wanting to get even with them people in Candelaria."

"It's not just them," Mitch said. "It's the Gunsmith. He's the one who killed both Jud and Ulysses. He's the one I'm going to see planted."

"Maybe *you're* the one that'll get planted."

Mitch looked the gunfighter straight in the eye. "Ulysses was faster than me and so was Jud. But they were foolish men, and too proud of their gun speed. Me, I'm smarter than the rest, and I'll come up with a way to trap the Gunsmith and kill him. You wait and see."

"What's in it for me?"

Mitch shrugged. "You said you wanted to go down in history, and the only way you could do it was to kill the Gunsmith. Well, this is your chance. The Gunsmith won't rest until he finds Molly. She's the bait for our trap."

"Some bait," Folsom said with a wink.

Mitch turned away and watched as Hank led his big gelding out of the wash, then saddled the animal. That done, the giant picked Molly up as easily as if she were a rag doll and tossed her across the saddle. He mounted behind her and waited for Mitch and Frank to pull their own saddles out of the buckboard and unhitch their horses.

"Damn good thing them saddle horses of yours pull a wagon," Hank drawled. "This big horse of mine wouldn't stand for it."

Molly felt Hank place his big hand on her butt and roughly massage it. His touch almost made her scream, and she knew she could not endure more of the same. "Ohhh," she groaned. "Ohhh, my head!"

"She's coming around," Hank said, taking his hand off her backside.

"Then sit her up, and let's not waste any more time," Mitch said.

Hank reined his horse to a standstill, then he dismounted and grabbed Molly and sat her up straight in the saddle. "Hey, woman. Sit up now, you hear."

Molly nodded as if dazed and sat up in the saddle. The giant remounted and wrapped his forearm around her waist, and then spurred his horse after the others. Hank's right hand rested on her thigh, and he immediately began to take liberties as he reined his horse with his left hand. Molly gritted her teeth and squeezed her eyes shut. She would have to endure this monster, and then she would be raped by the diseased thin man unless she managed to escape somehow.

A tear slid down her cheek. Her chances of escaping these three outlaws weren't as good as those of a snowball in hell. Then I'll just grab a gun or a knife and make them kill me before I can kill them first, she thought.

They rode hard all day, and it was late in the afternoon when Folsom reined his lathered horse to a standstill. "Up there," he said, pointing to a low set of barren-looking hills. "Just beyond that west ridge is a little valley, where the cabin sits."

Mitch removed his Stetson and sleeved his forehead dry. He lifted in his stirrups and twisted around to study their backtrail. Across the miles he could not even see a hint of dust. "You see anything back there?" he asked Hank with his eagle's eyes.

"Nothing," Hank said after a long moment.

"Good," Mitch said.

"I keep telling you they'll never pick up our trail," Folsom said. "For one thing, they'd have expected us to come on horses, not in a damn slow buckboard."

"If the Gunsmith could find us in Death Valley," Mitch said, looking at Molly, who appeared to be near the point of collapse, "I reckon he can find us about anywhere. Let's go on. It'll be dark by the time we get up in those hills and find that cabin."

The three men rode on, and it was dusk before they finally approached the little valley and cabin.

"Somebody is there!" Hank said.

Folsom was tired and irritable. "Well, it was empty

when Ed and I spent the night not more than two weeks
ago! Whoever it is had better clear out fast."

Molly felt a stirring of hope rise in her chest. Maybe
someone would realize she was being held captive, and
they'd help her escape, or at least tell someone of her
plight. But almost as if he could read her mind, Mitch said,
"If you so much as say one word to whoever is there, he's
a dead man. Is that understood?"

Molly dipped her chin in understanding.

"You remember that," Mitch said, "or the blood of whoever is in that cabin will be on your conscience."

They rode up to within fifty yards of the little cabin, and
the only thing they saw moving was a Mexican burro tied
to a stake driven into the ground.

"Hello in there!" Mitch called as Folsom slipped his
six-gun out of his holster and held it low and out of sight.

A moment later, a small, gray-bearded prospector edged
around the doorway with an old shotgun in his hands. "Get
on out of here!" he shouted. "This cabin is taken."

"Now what do we do?" Hank asked glumly.

"We've got to get him out of there," Folsom said. "Our
horses are in bad shape for lack of feed and water. Most of
these old prospectors can't hit anything beyond their
noses."

Mitch didn't believe a word of that. "If you feel ready to
put that notion to the test, then go ahead and charge him."

"No, thanks," Folsom said after a long minute.

Mitch scowled, then cleared his throat and shouted,
"Mister, we need water and feed for the horses. And the
woman we have with us is in bad shape."

"Nearest town is Silver Peak," the prospector called.
"Go straight east about forty miles."

Mitch curbed his anger. "Our horses won't last to carry
us that far," he called. "And neither will the young
woman."

The prospector hesitated. It was clear that he did not want strangers near the cabin, but equally clear that he was a man of some compassion for women and horses. "All right," he said after a long pause, "you can ride in slow and easy, but keep your hands in sight and away from your guns. Let your animals drink, and fill your canteens, then you got to skeedaddle!"

Folsom hissed, "Let's get in close and catch him in a crossfire."

"No, please," Molly said. "He's just an old man."

"So what?" Folsom swore in anger. "I'll die young. You think I give a damn about him?"

"Let's take this slow and easy," Mitch said, spurring his weary horse forward toward the spring, into which someone had jammed a stovepipe so that the hot, steaming water bubbled up and out of the ground to cool and leak downhill and fill a little pond that irrigated about three acres of grass.

Hank stayed put and let the two gunmen go in from the sides. When the prospector saw what was happening, he immediately raised his shotgun and cried, "That's far enough, you men!"

Folsom's patience had run out. He went for his gun, and he was so fast that the prospector did not have time to aim, but fired from waist level. The shotgun's blast dwarfed the report of the six-gun, and a huge cloud of white smoke belched from its muzzle.

Molly saw the prospector's shoulder blossom redly, but at the same moment Folsom jerked over his saddle as if on a wire. Folsom's horse bolted away in terror, and the gunfighter's pistol exploded once more as he struck the ground and lay still.

Everything happened very fast then from one moment to the next. Mitch's gun started barking, and the prospector staggered back through the doorway and vanished as Mitch threw himself from his horse, landing on his feet. The momentum sent him skidding into the side of the cabin.

The prospector slammed the door shut, and he must have barred it from inside, because when Mitch staggered erect, he threw his body against the door, but it would not open.

"Damn!" Mitch shouted, throwing his shoulder at the door a second time in sheer frustration and then jumping sideways as a shotgun blast punched through the wood, narrowly missing him. "Damn!"

Hank threw himself out of the saddle and took Molly with him. His big gelding shied away to join the other pair of loose horses. The little burro, caught up in the excitement, pulled its stake out of the ground and went braying off toward the hills, with the horses close behind.

Hank charged the cabin, but was driven back as the prospector opened fire from a shooting hole. Molly, suddenly realizing she had been forgotten in the confusion, jumped to her feet and ran after the horses.

"The horses!" Mitch shouted. "Goddammit, Hank, she's going for the horses!"

Molly was barefoot and the rocks and stickers were cutting her feet to pieces, but she did not care. If just one of the horses would stop running, she would have a chance of escape.

"Shoot her!" Mitch screamed. "Goddammit, shoot her!"

Molly turned around to see the giant running after her. Maybe it was the crimson of sunset, but Hank appeared red in the face and already winded. Molly suddenly realized that, though Hank was immensely powerful, that did not mean that he could run very fast or very far. Taking hope and ignoring the pain that was radiating up from the soles of her feet, Molly raced after the horses toward the sundown.

The horses might run all night, and they might stop any minute. But the sun wouldn't stop its hurried slide into the horizon, and day was turning to night. Not even the Pike brothers could stop that from happening.

"Shoot her!" Mitch screamed.

A bullet whip-cracked past her face, and Molly ran even harder. She could hear Mitch yelling at his brother, and she could even hear Hank's tortured breathing as he tried to overtake her.

Run! she thought, not daring to look over her shoulder again. Run!

TWENTY-FIVE

It was noon when word reached Clint that every square foot of Candelaria had been searched, and there was not a sign of the Pike brothers to be found anywhere.

Heck Jacobs approached Clint and said, "So what are we going to do?"

Clint had been asking himself the very same question. "I think we had better assume they left in a wagon and search the roads north and south."

Jacobs nodded his head, worried. "What about Molly?"

"She's a dead woman if we don't find her soon."

"At least you'll have a posse this time," the blacksmith said.

But, surprisingly, the Gunsmith didn't want a posse. "Is your shoulder all right now? Can you ride, fight, and shoot?"

"Try me," Jacobs said.

"All right, I will. You see, if we form a posse, there's

166

almost no way we're going to get near enough to Molly to
save her. Ten or fifteen horses and riders will raise a dust
trail that will be visible for miles. And I always worry
about some trigger-happy posseman opening fire. If that
happens they might hit Molly, or she'll be killed by the
Pikes."

"So you don't need a posse?"

Clint shook his head. "Not if our main concern is getting Molly back safe and sound."

"What are you going to tell these people?" Jacobs
asked. "They remember how you asked for their help the
first time and they chickened out. They're more than willing to make up for it now."

"I'm going to tell them the truth," Clint said, hopping
up on a wagon and raising his hands to catch their attention.

The townspeople crowded around Clint. After a night of
searching for tracks out in the brush, followed by a long
and frustrating morning of searching every inch of the big
mining town, they were dispirited and gritty-eyed.

"We've lost their trail," Clint said. "I don't have to tell
you that. But I'm going hunting for them."

"We're with you all the way!" a miner shouted.

Clint shook his head. "It won't work," he said. "As you
all know, they have abducted Molly Malloy. If they catch
sight of a posse on their backtrail, they'll kill her for sure.
So Heck Jacobs and I are going alone."

A groundswell of angry protest washed over them,
which did not surprise Clint because they had every right to
complain. When their anger simmered down, he said,
"There're still a few men among you who were either on
Judge Cotter's jury or else testified against the Pikes.
Those brave people are in danger until the Pike brothers are
dead or behind bars in Carson City. That's another good
reason why this town needs to remain on guard."

The crowd's reaction was mixed. Some of the younger men were pretty upset, but the cooler heads prevailed until there seemed to be a rough consensus that the Gunsmith knew what he was doing.

Clint saw Ruth in the crowd, and he smiled at her. She smiled back, although he could tell that she was concerned about his leaving. Speaking to her as well as to everyone else, Clint said, "We won't be back until the job is done. Until then, I want someone to form a protection committee that will watch Missus Eubanks and the others whose lives are in danger."

Almost at once, the crowd shifted its attention from Clint to those among itself who wanted to be in charge of the "protection committee." There were loud arguments as Clint stepped down from the wagon and moved through the crowd to Ruth's side. He no longer gave a damn if anyone noticed he and the widow standing close together.

"Ruth, always carry a gun," he said. "I don't think that they'll come back, but I can't be sure. Mitch is smart, and he's unpredictable."

"I'll be fine," she said.

Clint kissed her, and then turned and went for his horse. Heck Jacobs was already mounted, and when Clint was in the saddle, he dug down into his pockets for a coin and showed it to the blacksmith. "We know they had to have gotten away in a wagon," he said. "That means they either went north or south."

Clint flipped the coin high in the air. "Heads we ride south, tails we go north."

The coin dropped into the palm of his hand, and Clint glanced at it, shook his head, and then turned the coin over onto his wrist. "Tails," he said.

"It was heads," the blacksmith argued.

"Yeah," Clint admitted, "but then no sane man should

allow the flip of a coin to make his life choices. Better by far to trust to your instincts."

"And your instincts say to go north up this road?"

"That's right," Clint said. "And my instincts say they'll have ditched the wagon before daylight this morning. That means we're going to have to ride at least four hours not knowing if we chose the right direction or the opposite one."

When the blacksmith had no comment, Clint touched spurs to Duke's flanks and galloped out of town with Jacobs at his side. There was no point in telling the blacksmith just how worried he was that the Pike brothers had gone in exactly the opposite direction. Yet, after being a law man for a fair number of years, Clint had learned to rely heavily on his hunches. And right now, they told him that Mitch would be thinking about a posse led by the Gunsmith hunting him into Death Valley—so he'd take the opposite direction out of town.

It was late in the afternoon when they saw the wagon tracks veer sharply off the dirt road into the brush. Clint almost let out a whoop of relief as he spurred Duke up a wash and came to a sliding stop beside an abandoned buckboard.

"It's them, all right," he said, picking up Molly's blanket and drinking in the smell of her perfume.

Heck piled off his horse, his own spirits greatly lifted by this news. "I'm no tracker," he said, staring at the hoof and bootmarks all around the abandoned wagon. "You'll have to tell me what we have here."

Clint handed the man his reins and crouched to study the tracks. He moved around the wagon once and said, "Here's that big horse with the heel stops we had the whole town searching for last night. There's no question that Hank was here, too. Look at the size of this boot print."

Jacobs came over to study the print for a long moment. His face hardened, remembering how Hank Pike had nearly beat him to death in Candelaria. "I'd sure appreciate it if you'd let me have him for myself," Jacobs said quietly.

Clint looked up from the ground. "You want Hank?"

"Yeah."

"Why?"

"I never had a man whip me that way," Jacobs said. "I'd just like to have a chance to pay him back."

Clint straightened. Heck Jacobs was well over six feet and built like an ox, but he probably gave away a good fifty pounds and five inches in height to the giant. "Listen," Clint said. "When we catch up with them, the most important thing is to save Molly. I know you feel the same way. And to do that, we're most likely going to have to kill the Pike brothers, not fight them with our fists."

"I understand that," Jacobs said. "All I'm saying is that, if we do get the drop on them and get Molly free, then I want my chance."

Clint did not like the idea one bit, but it was obvious that Jacobs was determined to redeem himself, and that getting this opportunity was damned important.

"Molly first, and then, if we're all still standing when the gunsmoke clears, you can have your chance. But I don't have to tell you that a man the size of Hank Pike can break your neck or your back."

"Not if I break his first," Jacobs said.

Clint looked away and continued reading the signs. "Three men and three horses."

"What about Molly?"

"She's riding double," Clint said. "Probably on the big horse with Hank."

Jacobs made a strangling sound in his throat that brought Clint up short. "Listen," he said. "If you can't control yourself, I don't want you around when we overtake these men. Is that clear?"

Jacobs struggled and regained his control. "I'm sorry," he said. "But the very thought of that man handling Molly is enough to drive me crazy."

"Then don't think about it," Clint said. "Think of something else. Think of how good it will feel to hold that woman in your own arms."

Heck Jacobs nodded. "Yeah," he said. "So can we get moving?"

"Sure," Clint said, swinging into the saddle. "I just hope we have enough moonlight to follow these tracks. Fortunately, the ground is soft, and they have no reason to expect they are being followed, so the tracks are real clear."

TWENTY-SIX

Molly could not catch the horses, and she was too weak to go any farther. Somewhere behind her she could still hear Hank Pike stumbling around in the semi-darkness of the moonlight, while ahead of her she could see the three saddled horses trotting steadily across the broken, rocky ground.

Twice, Molly had felt sure she would catch a saddle-horse, but each time she had made her rush toward the weary, thirst-driven animals, they had bolted and raced away again. It was heartbreaking, and her feet were cut so badly that she knew she was not going to be able to go farther.

The desert night was filled with stars, and as she staggered after the horses, Molly thought about her past and what could have been her future with Heck Jacobs. Heck would have made a wonderful husband and father to

Annie. But now that life was gone. Hank would soon overtake her and probably, in his rage, kill her on the spot.

Molly saw the dark and humped outline of boulders just up ahead and staggered toward them. She slipped in between a pair of huge rocks and huddled in the darkness. Her mouth was cotton dry and her tongue so swollen from thirst that it almost choked her.

"Molly!" Hank shouted. "Goddamn you, Molly!"

She smiled and squeezed deeper into the rocks and found a crevasse through which she could see the man following her. Maybe she would die of thirst and heat, but maybe Hank would, too.

Hank seemed to grow out of the sage, and when he stopped he was less than a hundred yards from where she was hidden. Molly held her breath. She could see his massive silhouette sway with fatigue, and she noted how his shoulders slumped with defeat. He turned toward the rocks and looked directly at her. Molly froze and listened to her heartbeat until the giant staggered onward.

"Molly!" he bellowed. "You're gonna die out here without me!"

Good, she thought. Better death than ever to endure again what you had in mind.

Molly leaned her head back against the warm rocks and closed her eyes as Hank finally disappeared over the next ridge. She could still hear his ragged voice, but now he was no longer a part of her reality. The only physical things that registered in her mind were pain, the hard rocks that surrounded her, and the gradually slowing beat of her heart as she waited for death.

Hank was also beginning to consider the possibility of his own death. He knew that he and Mitch desperately needed their runaway horses as well as water to escape this land. Several hours ago he had been wondering how he could kill Frank Folsom so that he could have Molly the way he remembered when she was young and tender. Now the old prospector had killed Folsom. A prospector! And Molly was gone. Lost someplace out here and certain never to be found.

Hank wearily trudged up to the next ridge and tried to calm his feverish mind. He wondered if the goddamn horses would ever stop long enough for him to catch them.

It was Molly's fault. She was too dumb to understand that you couldn't rush a runaway animal or it would bolt and gallop off every time. Hell no, you couldn't! You had to move slow to a spooked horse. Talk to it in a nice, easy voice. Make it think that you weren't angry with it even though you wanted to kill the sonofabitch once you got your hands wrapped in its mane.

Hank came to a standstill. He saw the horses and the damned burro again, and they were less than a mile off and standing spraddle-legged with fatigue. They looked even worse than he felt. Hank's grin split his parched lips, but he did not care. For the first time in hours, hope stirred in his heart, and he trudged forward. He had been around horses all his life, and he understood their thinking better than he did the thinking of men.

"Easy, easy, easy," he said when he was still several hundred yards from the three skittish animals. The burro, much more rested and not at all thirsty, began to bray in alarm, and if the horses had been fresh, they'd have run for certain.

"Easy," Hank repeated. His own gelding nickered softly, and Hank smiled. "Thattaboy. You know me."

The horse, which had often been ill treated by the giant man, was suffering too much to do anything but come to its master.

Hank's fist snaked out and grabbed the animal's bit. It

was a wicked Spanish spade bit, and Hank twisted it hard; the gelding jumped back in pain, but the giant would not be shaken loose. He would like to have kicked the gelding a couple of times in the belly for all the damn trouble it had caused him, but he was afraid the big horse might break away, so instead, he tightened his cinch and mounted.

Just as Hank had expected, once he was in the saddle, the other two horses allowed themselves to be caught without any more fuss. Hank took their reins and led the spare horses back the way he'd come, and the damned burro trotted contentedly along behind. Hank figured that Mitch was probably still at the cabin and had killed the prospector by now. Maybe he and Mitch would slaughter the burro and roast its meat. Apache liked burro meat, and Hank reckoned he could stomach anything when he was starving.

Hank found Mitch trudging wearily along on his back-trail. "What the hell you doin' out here!"

"Without horses, we got nothing," Mitch growled.

"We got nothing without water, either," Hank said. "I thought you'd have killed the old man by now."

"I would have, except that I was worried about these horses. Besides, it'll be easier to take him with both of us coming at him from opposite sides. You saw what he did to Folsom. Where's Molly?"

Hank shook his head and handed reins to his brother. "I lost her in the dark."

"Damn!" Mitch cursed. "I had decided to use her as bait for the Gunsmith, and now . . . now we got nothing. We'll go looking for her tomorrow after we take the cabin from that sonofabitch with the shotgun."

"I think she'll be dead by tomorrow."

"So will these horses if we don't get them water, Mitch said, thinking about how bad things had started to turn for them.

They rode on for almost an hour before Mitch said, "You know what?"

"What?"

"We're having a streak of bad luck," Mitch said. "Ain't nothing has gone right since the day we robbed the bank and the Wells Fargo office and then ran into the Gunsmith."

"I know. So what?"

Mitch's brow furrowed. "I swear Jud and Ulysses will turn over in their graves if I say this, but I'm thinking that sometimes it's better to cut your losses and quit a game that goes sour."

Hank was not sure he understood. "You mean, just leave without paying them back?"

"It's just something I been thinking about tonight."

"I been thinking the same thing," Hank admitted. "I ain't ready to die, and things been going against us for a long time."

"Maybe the prospector has a bunch of gold in that cabin," Mitch said. "Maybe that's why he was so damn unfriendly."

Hank brightened. "Yeah! I'll bet it is!"

"We'll get him at daybreak, and then we'll search the place and water the horses. If we find gold, I think the thing to do is to head for California. Maybe the Barbary Coast. I hear they got some beautiful women over there, and the weather is always cool."

"It's most always hot here," Hank said. "And I sure wish we had Molly to pleasure ourselves with before we rode on. I was gonna kill Folsom before I'd let him use Molly first."

Mitch looked at his brother. "Funny thing you should say that, because I was thinking along those same lines. I never liked him anyway. I reckon the prospector did us a favor by killing Frank."

Hank knuckled his swollen eyes. "I'm going to need some shut-eye before we ride to California. A couple of hours at least. We ain't had a decent night's sleep in three days."

"All right," Mitch said. "We'll kill the prospector, then sleep and eat, then see if we can track down Molly."

"What for?" She's likely dead."

"But if she isn't," Mitch said, "we can pay our last respects for old times' sake."

Hank barked a laugh, and the two rode on through the warm summer night.

TWENTY-SEVEN

Clint shoved his boot into his stirrup and mounted Duke. To the east, he saw the first light of dawn seeping into the retreating nighttime darkness. He twisted in the saddle and looked toward the low hills just off to his right. "Tracks lead straight up there," he said. "Unless I miss my guess, that's where we'll find them."

Heck Jacobs followed his gaze to the nearby hills. "And water, I hope?"

"Yeah," Clint said, pushing Duke toward the hills at an easy trot. "There had better be water, or we're all in trouble."

They were treated to a spectacular desert sunrise. The sky turned faintly salmon and then brilliant red, streaked by wispy clouds of spun gold. The Gunsmith was halfway up the side of the barren hills when he heard the first gunshots.

"Let's go!" he said, spurring Duke up the trail.

The going was tough and the footing was poor, but both horses performed well, and when they topped the last rise, the Gunsmith saw a small, grassy valley, a cabin, and corrals, and then he saw Mitch and the giant Hank Pike exchanging fire with someone in the cabin. The brothers were still a good mile away, but it was clear that whoever was in the cabin had about run out of time, because the Pike brothers were closing for the kill.

"I got Hank," the blacksmith said, whipping his horse forward.

Clint couldn't have stopped Heck Jacobs if he'd tried. So instead of protesting, he charged Mitch and covered nearly five hundred yards before the two brothers were even aware that they were being attacked.

The giant bolted toward his horse as Jacobs came roaring down on him. Realizing that he could not reach his horse, Hank unleased two shots; one of them struck the blacksmith's horse and brought it down. Heck Jacobs was thrown over his animal's head, but he landed in a pile of sagebrush, which broke his fall. The blacksmith took cover and returned fire.

Clint's attention was grabbed when one of Mitch's bullets creased his saddle. The Gunsmith, afraid that Duke would be hit again, piled off his horse and charged the gunman on foot. He did not come straight at the man, but moved from side to side. Mitch was cool, and he did not turn and run as his brother had, but instead aimed and fired, each bullet just missing Clint.

The Gunsmith stopped, leveled his revolver at eye level, and shouted, "Drop it!"

Mitch didn't listen, and when his hammer struck empty, he reached for his cartridge belt and pulled out some fresh bullets and began to reload.

"Drop it, I said!"

But Mitch Pike had no intention of surrendering as he

worked, frantically ejecting spent cartridges and ramming in fresh ones.

Clint cocked back the hammer of his pistol and said, "If you don't drop the gun, I'll shoot."

Now, for the first time, Mitch smiled. "Just shoot to kill, you sonofabitch! I ain't facing no Carson City hangman!"

When Mitch finished loading and cocked his gun, Clint fired. His bullet caught Mitch in the right forearm and shattered it. The man's gun flew out of his hand, and he sagged to his knees, screaming with a mixture of fury and pain. "I told you to kill me!" he shouted.

"I don't take orders from murderers, nor do I show them any more mercy than they showed their victims," Clint said, stepping over to kick the man's gun far out of his reach.

A grunt and a scream pulled him around in time to see the two huge titans locked in each other's arms, each attempting to break the other's back. Clint started to raise his gun, but decided there was much too great a risk of hitting Heck Jacobs to take a chance.

"Hank will break him like a sapling," Mitch spat, holding his arm.

"Don't count on it." The Gunsmith watched as the two men strained and swayed, their faces red and their huge biceps bulging with exertion. Suddenly, Hank managed to trip the blacksmith and they crashed to the earth. Involuntarily, Jacobs bellowed in pain and, for an instant, Clint thought the blacksmith was finished.

But Jacobs wasn't finished. He abandoned his bearhug and used his big fists to pound Hank in the face until the giant's nose broke. Hank shouted and tried to turn his face away, but two more blows caught him squarely, and he released the blacksmith, then started to climb to his feet.

Jacobs tackled the bigger man, and this time he used his head to slam into Hank's chin and mouth. Even Clint winced to see how the giant's head violently snapped back and forth. It seemed impossible that Hank's neck did not break.

The two men crawled to their feet; Heck did not give the giant time to wipe the blood from his eyes. He came in swinging from all angles. It wasn't pretty fighting, but each blow made Hank grunt and retreat a step. The blacksmith was like a crazy man as he bludgeoned Hank Pike until the giant just folded at the knees and sagged to the ground, covering his battered face.

"That's enough!" Clint shouted. "He's beaten!"

Heck Jacobs' face was wild with hatred as he grabbed the beaten outlaw by the shirtfront and shook him. "Where is she?" he bellowed. "What did you do to her?"

Hank couldn't speak. He was covered with gore and having trouble breathing. Clint had to snatch Mitch's gun and run over to pull Jacobs away from the beaten giant.

"Killing him isn't going to help us find Molly," he said.

Heck threw his arm out and knocked Clint a foot backward, but then he seemed to realize what he was doing. "I'm sorry, Clint," he said. "I lost my head for a few minutes."

"I understand," the Gunsmith said. He looked at the almost unrecognizable Hank Pike. "Where is Molly?"

"I don't know," Hank wheezed, wiping his face with his sleeve. "She ran away and died out there someplace."

Jacobs lunged for the man, but Clint managed to throw himself between them. "Stop it!" he shouted. "You've got to watch these two while I try to find her!"

"The hell with them!" Jacobs shouted. "Kill them both and be done with it. I'm going with you to find her."

The door to the shack opened up, and a grizzled-looking old prospector stepped outside with his shotgun. "I reckon

I owe you boys my life. I'll watch over this pair."

Clint sized up the prospector and liked what he saw.
Besides, any man who could hold off the Pikes with nothing but an old shotgun was not to be trifled with.

"All right," Clint said. "But first, I'll hogtie them."

He quickly tied the Pike brothers, and then he said to
Mitch, "If you didn't kill her, she might still be alive.
You're going to hang, but why have the death of a woman
on your conscience?"

"Why not!" Mitch spat.

Clint turned to the beaten giant, who seemed to be in
a state of shock. No doubt, Hank Pike had never re-
ceived the kind of physical beating he'd so often administered to smaller men. Clint knew that he would be no
help.

Clint addressed the prospector. "Did you see them come
in this morning?"

"Yeah, I seen 'em all right. That fool burro of mine ran
away with their horses last night. You follow his tracks,
they'll take you where you want to go."

"Thanks," Clint said. Looking at Heck Jacobs, whose
face and hands were skinned up, he said, "Your horse is
finished, but you can ride one of theirs. Let's water them
and ride."

Heck did not need to be asked twice. They and the
horses drank deeply of the cool water down by the pond.
Clint refilled their canteens and water bags, and then they
headed out toward the burro. It took Clint only a few minutes to pick up the tracks he wanted, and they rode hard to
the north into even tougher country than they'd already
traveled.

During the next few hours they did not speak at all.
Heck's eyes swelled up so that he was looking out of
purple-colored slits, but the man wasn't thinking about

his physical pain; every thought he had left was about Molly.

It was midday when they found her asleep under the rocks with a rattlesnake coiled not more than a yard from her bare and bloody feet.

"Don't move," Clint hissed, drawing his gun and taking aim.

When he fired, the snake's head disappeared, and the headless body began to writhe wildly in the sand. Heck jumped forward and scooped up the woman in his arms, and she awoke. For an instant, a scream formed in her throat, and then she recognized Heck and threw her arms around his bull neck.

Clint stepped out of the rocks and holstered his gun. He heard the woman and the man both start to cry; it was a good sound, an alive sound.

The Gunsmith went down to their waiting horses and unstrapped their canteens. As soon as she was well enough to travel, Heck would take Molly back to Candelaria, but Clint would escort the Pike brothers on to Carson City, where justice would finally be served by a hangman's noose. Then he would ride back to tell the people of Candelaria they would never again have to live in fear, because they would stand and fight.

And after all that, he'd tell those people they were just going to have to do without a Wells Fargo office, because he was taking Ruth the hell out of this damned desert, at least until the mountain aspen turned the colors of this morning's sunrise.

Watch for

HANDS OF THE STRANGLER

97th in the exciting GUNSMITH series
from Jove

coming in January!

J.R. ROBERTS
THE
GUNSMITH